HER MOMENT
IN THE SPOTLIGHT

HER MOMENT IN THE SPOTLIGHT

BY

NINA HARRINGTON

MILLS & BOON

First published in Great Britain 2011
by Mills & Boon, an imprint of Harlequin (UK) Limited,
Large Print edition 2011
Eton House, 18-24 Paradise Road,
Richmond, Surrey TW9 1SR

© Nina Harrington 2011

ISBN: 978 0 263 22231 9

Harlequin (UK) policy is to use papers that are natural,
renewable and recyclable products and made from
wood grown in sustainable forests. The logging and
manufacturing process conform to the legal environmental
regulations of the country of origin.

Printed and bound in Great Britain
by CPI Antony Rowe, Chippenham, Wiltshire

CHAPTER ONE

MIMI FIORINI RYAN picked up the poster for London Fashion Weekend and scanned down the list of events until she came to a small paragraph of elegant bold script, which encapsulated her entire future in a few short lines and sent her heart racing:

Langdon Events is proud to present an exclusive fashion show in aid of the Tom Harris Foundation for Climbing for the Disabled.

The New Classics collection from Studio Designs will be introduced by their head designer, Mimi Ryan, one of London's brightest new talents.

Tickets selling fast.

The words were almost swimming in front of her. Mimi had to blink several times to clear her head and come to terms with the fact that she was awake, and that this was not a dream.

'Well, what do you think? You look a bit stunned.'

Poppy Langdon leant across the desk and bared her teeth. 'Do you hate it? Because I'm not sure I can change anything with only a week to go.'

Did she hate it—hate the fact that, after ten years of study and working every evening and weekend, she finally had a chance to show her clothing designs to the public? *Hate it?*

Mimi grinned at the bubbly blonde. She had only known her for a few weeks but she was rapidly becoming a good friend whom Mimi felt able to trust with something as important as the organisation of her dream fashion show.

'No—I don't hate it. It's just that…'

'Go on. I can take it,' Poppy whimpered. 'Tell me now and get it out of your system.'

Mimi coughed a reply and shook her head for a second before coming round to the other side of the desk and hugging Poppy warmly before grinning down at her.

'It's just that I have been working towards this day for a very long time. It means so much to me,

I can't tell you. Thank you so much for giving me a chance. I don't *hate* it at all—I *love* it.'

Poppy breathed out a sigh of relief and hugged her back.

'You are welcome—but I should be the one who is thanking you! If you hadn't stepped in last month I wouldn't have a charity fashion show at all. You are going to be a total hit! I predict it now. We have already sold loads of tickets, so you can stop worrying and start enjoying yourself.'

Poppy grinned and crinkled her nose. 'Even if we are in the middle of a heat wave,' she added, flicking her long hair away from her neck. 'Why is it so hot in June? And how do you manage to always look so cool and elegant in black?'

Mimi took a breath and tried to answer Poppy without betraying the inner turmoil.

If only Poppy knew how very hard Mimi had worked to look so cool and elegant. It was all about looking the part on the outside. From the black trouser-suit that had taken her a week to tailor down to her simple mocha-silk tee and antique gold wrist-watch she had inherited from her mother. Every breath Mimi Fiorini Ryan took was totally focused on one thing: persuading Poppy

Langdon that she had made the right decision to use Mimi's first clothing collection as part of her charity fashion show.

'Me?' Mimi replied, glancing down at her wide-leg trousers and loose top. 'Natural fibres, I suppose—and I am indoors most of the time.' She paused then tilted her head. 'How is the iced coffee?'

'Divine!' Poppy replied with a warm smile, fanning herself with a brochure and shrugging up her shoulders in delight. 'I had no idea there was an Italian bistro just around the corner. You are so resourceful!'

'Not really. My parents and I used to come to this part of London a lot when I was at college. I'm just pleased that the bistro is still here and the coffee is as good as ever.'

Poppy saluted her with the cup. 'Nectar. Seeing as you are a total life-saver, I do have one final treat for you.' She took one last long slurp then started sorting through the stacks of folders on her desk. 'The hotel has come back to me with a few ideas for the catwalk part of the show. I know you want elegant and sophisticated, and the hotel ballroom is just perfect, but we do need to confirm how much space we need before they start renovation work on the rest of the hotel. Can you stay a little longer?'

Mimi could only chuckle at that question. She would happily stay here for the rest of the week if Poppy would put up with her.

'Of course. But here's an idea—why don't I pop out for refills on the coffee? I'll be right back...'

If there had been an Academy award for 'leading man in your own drama', then Hal Langdon would have been determined to head the list of nominees.

Hal swung himself out of the London black cab with the help of the hand rail, his one crutch and a special sideways slide-and-stand motion which had taken him weeks to perfect in the numerous ambulance trips between his chalet in the French Alps and the local hospital.

Pain shot through his left leg as soon as he shifted his weight from the crutch onto the ankle wrapped in an inflatable boot. The thrill of finally being free of the heavy plaster-cast which had protected what was left of his smashed ankle and broken leg had soon faded when he'd realised just how far he still had to go before he could walk on his own.

But that was what he was going to do.

One slow, faltering, painful step at a time.

He was going to prove to the world that he could walk again—and perhaps convince himself at the same time.

It was all about going forward and pretending to the outside world that his old life was not a total sham, while his new life was as yet a complete mystery.

The doctors had made it clear: no more climbing, no more high-risk sports, no more doing the job which had taken him all over the world filming the more exciting experiences an adrenaline junkie could find on this planet.

And in his heart and gut he knew that they were right. Not just because his body was no longer capable of taking that amount of relentless punishment month after month, year after year, but because of something more important.

The day that he had lost his climbing partner was the day that his old life had ended.

Tom Harris had saved his life more than once since their first crazy adventures at university. Tom had been his best friend, the older brother he'd never had.

And now Tom was dead, killed in a fall that Hal relived in Technicolor detail every night in his dreams, and was reminded of every single time he looked at his leg or felt the ridge on his head where he had fractured his skull. It had been five months, but the memory of those terrible few minutes on the mountain was still as fresh as yesterday. Just as vivid; just as painful; just as traumatic.

And some part of Hal had died that day too.

This made his decision to come back to London and work on the charity Tom had founded both logical and ridiculous at the same time. Every time Tom's name was mentioned it was like an ice-axe going into his gut again.

But what else could he do? He was the one who had suggested to Tom that the events company he'd created with his sister should organise a fundraising event for the work with disabled climbers that Tom had become passionate about during the last year of his life.

It was little wonder that Poppy had telephoned him to ask when he was planning to arrive to help her with the arrangements, claiming that she was snowed under with other work she desperately needed to spend time on. His sister certainly knew which buttons to press to bring on even more guilt. It had been his decision to leave Poppy to run the company on her own while he had enjoyed the life of action and excitement he had always yearned for during the years they had spent building up the company together.

But it was more than that, and she knew it.

He was expected to be at the fundraiser, both as Tom's friend and as the co-founder of Langdon Events—even if that meant that he would have to endure the constant reminders of the man Tom had been.

He would survive the next week in the same way that he had survived the last five months: one day at a time. Each day was filled with the confused feelings of anger and resentment at the way Tom had died blended with his own overwhelming feeling of failure and the endless self-recriminations.

He had to start taking action and getting back into some sort of work—otherwise he would be guilty of failing Tom all over again.

Head back, chin up, chest forward, Hal glanced at the huge plate-glass doors that marked the entrance to the elegant stone building where Langdon

Events rented a second-floor office. He gave a low chuckle and shook his head in disgust.

There were three flights of steep stone steps between the pavement and the entrance. He knew that there was a ramp at the back of the building, but he had not spent his life leading from the front to use the disabled entrance now, even if his sister Poppy did call him stubborn. He was determined to negotiate the steps leading up to the front entrance just like he had before.

Hal Langdon looked up at the glass doors, clenched his fingers tight around the rubber grip of his crutch and braced his jaw even tighter.

Just as Hal was about to take that first step with his good right leg, he was distracted by a flash of movement from inside the building; a few seconds later the glass doors slid open. A pretty girl skipped down the steps onto the pavement, and in seconds was on the other side of the road.

Her attention was so fixed on her target that she had not even glanced once in his direction. He watched in amusement as she weaved her way through the bustling crowds and clusters of tourists who flocked to this part of Covent Garden.

She was clearly a girl on a mission.

He could not resist a smirk at the way she ducked and dived from side to side, onto the road then back onto the pavement, shoulder-bag tight across her chest, elbows tucked into her sides. Her face was totally focused on the goal—so focused that she probably did not realise that she was biting her lower lip in concentration and that her reddish-brown hair was flying up around her pale face.

Black trousers and a coffee-coloured blouse could not disguise a great figure—and also a tanta-lising glimpse of a shapely ankle above shoes with the kind of heels Poppy would kill for. Someone somewhere must be in desperate need of coffee to send this poor girl out on a mission in that outfit in what passed for a warm day in London.

He was almost disappointed when she turned the corner and was immediately swallowed up out of view. *Good for you*, he acknowledged with a twist of his upper lip. *Mission accomplished.*

Time to find out if some of that sense of purpose would rub off on him.

Ten minutes later he stepped out of the elevator, his ankle still aching with the effort, his T-shirt damp with perspiration. He steadied himself for a few minutes to cool off, before taking the few steps to the office he had last seen over a year ago.

Not much had changed, not even the small blonde girl sitting with her head down behind the wide partners' desk they had bought with such enthusiasm all those years ago so that they could work together from the same office.

Buying such an enormous desk had seemed like a good idea at the time.

Now she looked tiny, and swamped by the stacks of boxes and folders which seemed to cover every flat space in the room.

A twinge of guilt heightened the tension in his shoulders. She was overworked and would probably have asked him back even earlier if it had not been for his injury.

He shuffled on his crutch and her head lifted. 'Oh, that was fast, Mimi. How did you manage to...? Hal!' Poppy squealed and flung herself out of her chair and into his chest, her knee connecting with his leg as she pressed against him.

'Ouch!' He flinched and hugged her back, one-handed.

'Sorry,' she replied and ducked her head. 'Your leg; I had forgotten for a minute.'

Then she stood back with her hands on her hips and slowly shook her head. 'Something is definitely different about you today.' She pretended to scan him from head to toe. 'Is it the hair—which is desperate for a restyle, by the way? Or perhaps the jacket? No?'

Hal snorted and Poppy laughed, stepped forward and kissed him warmly on the cheek.

'That boot may not win many fashion awards but it is certainly a big improvement on the horrible cast. You look a lot better.'

Then she play-thumped him on the arm. 'You pest! I should be annoyed at you. Why didn't you tell me you were coming? I could have picked you up at the airport—made a fuss of you.'

'You mean apart from the fact that you have a bucket-seat sports car built for one tiny person and their handbag?'

'Well, yes, apart from that small detail.' Poppy waved her arm towards the office chair and Hal lowered himself into it very slowly, leg out in front of him. The office was so small that Poppy had to step over his leg to reach her chair.

'Tell me everything, big brother. How is France? How long can you stay? Because, in case you haven't noticed, I am swamped. Oh—and you know that you are always welcome *chez moi*; my pals would love to see you. They are totally into cosseting and, darling, you need some serious love and care. What? What?'

Hal held up one hand in surrender.

'Please can I have a word in edgeways? Okay. France is great but I've rented out the chalet and put my stuff into storage. I am staying long enough to get through Tom's fundraiser, then we can see what I can do to help you with that workload. And, thank you, I would love to sleep on your couch. But no cosseting. I've had more than enough cosseting these last few months.'

'Wow,' Poppy replied in a low voice and sat back. 'Now you have surprised me. You love that chalet. What made you rent it out?'

Hal inhaled a couple of deep breaths before even trying to reply.

Back in France the Langdon Events team had protected him from the press, the media and whoever else wanted the inside story on how Tom Harris had died. Did they really think that he had not noticed how they almost took shifts to make sure that there was always someone there when he woke in the night? How they had started to fuss over him when he was finally out of a wheelchair and onto crutches and something close to being mobile? That they were guarding him, as though he could not be allowed to be alone?

After five months he had felt trapped, enclosed by walls which seemed to be pressing down on him, desperate to be free from the constant pressure to talk about Tom. Desperate to heal.

Hal looked into Poppy's eyes and he could see her happy expression fall away. They had been close once, but he had pushed her back to London the minute he'd left hospital. There was so much he wanted to tell her, but that was impossible without breaking his word to Tom, and his frustration was too fierce to inflict on anyone else. Poppy deserved better than that.

'This is all about Tom, isn't it?' She asked in a low voice. 'You couldn't stand to be living in the same village where Tom and Aurelia used to live. Oh, Hal. I am so sorry.'

'Too many reminders.' He shrugged. 'I needed some time away. The team back in France can run the events programme without me getting in their way.'

His crutch tapped gently against the side of his boot. 'The cast is off and I'm ready to get back to work, even if I am barred from anything even vaguely sporty.' He grinned across at her. 'But right now I have to get through this fundraiser next weekend. It was my idea, and the sponsors will expect me to be there. So now it is your turn to tell me everything. What grandiose schemes for world domination are you working on these days?'

'Ah. That, my darling brother, is one of the many reasons I called to check that you were mobile. I need your help and I need it now.'

Mimi lifted her precious cargo of iced coffee over the heads of a pair of tourists who were too busy huddled around their guide book to notice that they were blocking her path. She did not relax until she reached the safety of Poppy's office building.

The heat and the stress of the last few weeks were beginning to kick in.

Of course, Poppy did not need to know that Mimi had only finished off the final piece of crystal work on the nude-pink floor-length evening gown at two that morning.

She had been so busy organising the end-of-year

show for her students at the local fashion college; it had been a real struggle to squeeze in the time for such delicate work outside shop hours. Finding the perfect crystals and creating the embellishment on the bodice had taken her weeks of hand sewing but it had been worth it. The gown was stunning, even if she said so herself, and the final garment was ready seven days before the show.

Her first fashion show. Her first collection of clothing she had designed and made herself.

It was so close that she could almost touch it. A week; that was all. Seven days!

This was the chance she had been longing for during the dark days of the last few years when a career as a fashion designer had seemed like a distant dream meant for other people, not girls who ran knitting shops while grieving for a lost parent in an unfashionable part of London.

Just the thought of it give her an instant zing of energy, and she practically skipped all the way back to Poppy's office.

She was just about to push open the door with her foot when she heard Poppy's distinctive light laughter, which was immediately followed by a very male voice.

Her hand froze as her brain worked through the options. It was a lovely sunny, warm Friday evening. Perhaps Poppy was going out for dinner or had a date? And why not? She had been working so hard these last few weeks; Poppy deserved to be spoilt. And they were running late. Perhaps it would be better if she took the plans with her back to the shop and left Poppy to enjoy her evening.

Mimi knocked with her knuckles on the door and pushed it open a little wider.

Poppy was still sitting at her desk, but sprawled across the whole length of the small office, and blocking her path to the desk, were the long denim-clad legs of a man who looked like a fashion stylist's idea of a playboy biker. Except that one of his legs was wearing a casual training-shoe while the other was encased from toes to knee in what looked like a surgical-support boot.

Conscious that she was staring at his leg, Mimi looked up into his face just as he turned to face her. Two dark-brown eyes gazed at her so intently that she almost blushed under the fierce heat of that focus.

He could have passed for a male model for the fashion show if it was not for the crutch leaning against Poppy's desk and the distinctive thin, white scar which curved across his forehead and down one side of his temple. And the dark, heavy eyebrows which made him look almost fierce.

His well-used black-leather jacket was stylish rather than beaten up and cut so as to accentuate the broad shoulders and slim waist beneath the T-shirt.

All blended with something more intangible, something which had nothing to do with the ego of a male model.

He had not said one word but in those eyes and that face she saw something powerful, at the same time quiet and deep.

This man filled the small office with his presence. Not in an intimidating way; far from it. She simply recognised that this was someone who knew what it was like to give instructions and have them followed to the letter. He was authoritative, commanding and probably the most handsome man she had seen in a very long time. Most definitely not the kind of man who came into her knitting shop.

He could be Poppy's date, but everything about him screamed power, position and authority. He had to be one of Poppy's other clients, one of the influential, powerful ones who paid her large fees to manage their corporate events so that she could afford to run charity fundraisers.

Poppy laughed out loud in delight at something he had said, whoever he was, lifted her head to face Mimi and waved at her to come in.

'Mimi; perfect timing. I need your help. I've just been trying to persuade my brother Hal here to work with us on the fashion show, and he is pretending to be reluctant.'

'Oh, no. I haven't forgotten all of the fashion events I organised when you were working as a model and we were struggling to get this company off the ground. I think it put me off for life,' he replied as he glanced back from Mimi to Poppy. 'Now, if you need a photographer, that I can help you with.'

Her brother!

Mimi's body locked into a 'half in the corridor, half in the room' position. She simply could not move. It was as though her feet were bolted to the carpet tiles. Just as firmly her eyes found something deeply fascinating in the cardboard tray she was still holding so tightly that it had started to develop a definite wobble. She dared not turn around or move one step forward.

It was his voice, of course, deep, husky and sensual—and just about as far away from the voices that she heard in her ordinary life. All she could do was stay rooted to the spot, feeling slightly stunned as the whirlwind of masculine energy twirled around her.

Oblivious to her predicament, Poppy reached forward with one arm and hugged Hal with a beaming grin. 'I might take you up on that. There is still a lot to do behind the scenes, and we have a list of events over the next few weeks where I am desperate for a photographer I can rely on. But this week I need help with the show. What can we do to convince you to get involved?'

'Would iced coffee help?' Mimi finally managed to squeak out as she inched forward a little closer to the desk, terrified that she was going to spill coffee over her precious plans or Hal Langdon's knees.

Only then did Poppy give a dramatic sigh. 'Oh, fantastic! And now I am being horribly rude. Hal, this is the fashion designer who is working with us for Tom's charity fundraiser next week. Mimi, meet my brother, Hal, the other half of Langdon Events.'

She cursed her vivid imagination. Mimi's attention was riveted by the sounds created by leather sliding against leather, the crunch of his boot and the scrape of the crutch on the carpet as he pulled his leg back, slid his left arm into the crutch and heaved himself to his feet. All set against the gentle whirring from the desk fan, which was totally failing to cool her hot neck. Her hair felt clammy and damp against her neckline. Not her best look when she was trying to impress her events manager—or that manager's brother.

'Oh, please don't get up,' Mimi said, and stepped forward just as Hal bent and stretched out his right hand towards her.

Only the gap between them was too close, and as she half-turned to shake hands she could not avoid colliding with the solid mass of his muscular frame and the crutch.

Her cardboard tray tilted as it was crushed between them, and it was only at the very last minute that Mimi's brain kicked into action and her arm whipped out sideways to prevent an explosion of iced coffee.

Her plan almost succeeded.

The tray stayed intact, but in the sudden movement a trickle of coffee escaped over the top of the ill-fitting plastic lid of one of the cups, dribbled down over the tray and onto her foot, soaking through her thin stocking and into her favourite black shoes.

As Mimi gasped in horror, it took a few seconds for her to realise that Hal had taken hold of her arm and was physically holding her steady. As she looked up from her damp shoe into his handsome face, he frowned and said in a low voice, 'I am so sorry. That was very clumsy of me. Are you okay?'

Standing only inches away from his body, she was very much aware of the remarkable, over-whelming masculinity of this man. If she inhaled deeply their bodies would be pressed together chest to chest. He smelt of dust, man sweat and something fragrance manufacturers had been trying to capture and bottle for decades without success: masculine energy and drive, with a shot of pure attraction and goodness knew how many phero-mones.

It was a heady combination that many women would save up to be able to afford—and she was one of them. This magical aroma, combined with the sensation of the rough skin of his fingertips on the back of her arm, sent a shiver of totally shocking but delightful anticipation and sensory pleasure through her body and robbed her of speech.

'Fine. Not a problem,' she eventually managed to say. 'No damage done.' And she braved a small smile before slipping out away from his grasp and lowering her tray to the safety of Poppy's desk.

Poppy looked across to Mimi with a shake of the head. 'Ignore my brother, Mr Famous Mountaineer, outdoor man. It's the bungee jumping, you know. High Altitudes. Affects the brain.'

'I like to think of myself as the overseas section of the company.' Hal smiled at Mimi with a gentle nod, his eyes locked onto her face. It was not a casual glance but a stare so deliberate and focused she felt uncomfortable under the hard, bright heat of it. His heavy, dark eyebrows were squeezed together as though he had recognised her from somewhere and was trying to place her.

One thing was certain—if she had met Hal Langdon before, she would certainly have remembered.

'Pleased to meet you, Miss…?'

Swallowing down a nervous lump the size of Scotland, Mimi managed to croak out, 'Ryan. Mimi Ryan,' only a second before Hal turned back to Poppy, who was sighing in exasperation as he spoke.

'You should be,' Poppy sniffed. 'Mimi has had to drop everything to pull together her first collection in time for the show next weekend. It's going to be a huge success, and bring in tons of cash for Tom's charity, but we are not there yet. Still loads to do. So be nice to poor Mimi.'

Hal stood in silence for a few seconds before sitting down with legs outstretched on the corner of the desk. His bottom covered Mimi's poster and her floor plan, ruining any chance she might have of grabbing them and making a run for it.

'Here's a suggestion.' His fingers seemed to tighten around the grip inside his crutch. 'Seeing as I am well and truly grounded at the moment, why don't I make myself useful on some of the other projects we have going? That way you can focus on the fundraiser while I...'

But before he could finish his sentence, Hal's voice was drowned out by the loud ringing of the desk telephone and then Poppy's mobile phone only seconds later.

Poppy took one glance at the caller identity, sucked in air between her teeth, mouthed the word 'Sorry,' then picked up the phone.

'Hello, Maddy. How are you and…? Oh. Well, I'm very sorry to hear that. Did you talk to…? And then what did she say? Now, Maddy, I need you need to calm down just for a second. Take a deep breath, that's it. Inhale slowly. Well done. Now, start at the beginning—why exactly do you want me to cancel your wedding?'

Seconds stretched to minutes as Poppy scribbled down notes and made sympathetic noises down the phone until her eyes closed and she splayed out her fingers across her forehead.

'It's all going to be fine. I can catch a flight to Florence tonight and we can have a breakfast meeting in the morning and sort the whole thing out. Yes, I know the hotel. See you tomorrow, Maddy. I know, I know. Bye for now.'

In the stunned silence that followed, Mimi looked from Poppy, who had her head in her hands, to Hal, who pushed himself up off the desk so that he was facing Poppy.

'Did I just hear you say that you were going to Italy?' he asked, his voice low, deep and resonant. 'Please tell me that I am mistaken.'

'There's no point scowling at me like that!' And then her shoulders sagged. 'Do you remember that French redhead I worked with in Marrakech? The one you said had even less dress-sense than my other model pals?'

'Was that the one who pushed me into the pool when I said that she looked skinny in a sarong?'

Poppy nodded. 'That's the one. Well, she is supposed to be getting married to a very charming and very wealthy Italian aristocrat in Florence in three weeks and Langdon Events is planning their wedding.'

Hal raised his eyebrows. 'Poppy the wedding planner? How sweet.'

She inhaled deeply. 'Do not mock. Some of us like weddings, and the income pays for this office. The problem is that I thought there would be plenty of time to produce the charity show then move on to the wedding, but the woman is driving me crazy. They have already changed the venue and reception menu twice. That call was the final straw. Apparently her mother hates the church and venue, and has now decided that she is allergic to all of the food on the menu for the reception and that it would be far better for her to take over the wedding plans herself and move the wedding to Paris.'

Poppy shook her head. 'I cannot change the wedding arrangements, not now, but this is not the kind of discussion I can have over the phone. I need to be on a flight to Italy tonight if there is any chance of saving this wedding. Maddy is relying on me to create the perfect wedding she's always dreamt about, and I promised her that I would do the very best I could to make that dream come true. I can't let her down now.'

Poppy sat back in her chair, her fingernails tapping out a fast beat on the table for a few seconds before they paused and she looked up across at Hal with a mischievous grin. 'If only I could find someone to take over the fashion show and run the office for a few days while I am in Florence. I would *hate* for any last-minute problems in London to ruin the event.'

Mimi turned back to face Hal, who instead of sympathising and offering immediate assistance had folded his arms and was staring at Poppy with his eyebrows raised.

'Poppy, darling. I know you far too well. I smell a plan being put into action here where I am shanghaied and sold down the river without a word to say about it. Could this wedding be the *real* reason why the normally super-efficient Poppy Langdon called me from my sick bed in France? Have you been planning this all along?'

She looked at him, fluttered her eyelids a couple of times and smiled sweetly. 'Me? Well, that would be very devious of me, wouldn't it? Either way, now that you are going to be working full time, it seems to me that you have arrived just in time to save the day, big brother. Congratulations, Hal—you are now the official organiser for the Tom Harris Foundation fundraiser and fashion show. Isn't that wonderful news?'

CHAPTER TWO

MIMI reached across and tugged at the pristine linen tablecloth so that the edge was perfectly aligned along the length of her old family breakfast table.

As her fingers ran along the fine fabric, she was taken back to a warm summer evening when both of her parents had been alive. They had decided over a stunning Italian *al fresco* dinner on the patio to embroider a full set of table linen with bright flowers and yellow swallowtail butterflies so that they could enjoy a taste of summer over a cold, grey London winter.

Mimi had offered to help with the tablecloth as a diversion from her university design-work. In the end her mother had given in because they were so busy in the shop that the napkins would be easier for them to work in the few spare minutes between customers.

Four napkins—*four*. That was all her mother had managed to complete before the telephone call that had summoned her back to Milan and the Fiorini family. And after that? Somehow there had seemed little point. The joy had left their lives.

Yet it seemed so right to bring out this tablecloth to help celebrate her mother's birthday. Celebrating her birthday every year was just one of the many promises by Mimi that her mother had insisted on in her lucid moments, such as making sure that she kept the knitting shop solvent—and taking every chance she could to prove that she was a professional fashion designer who could stand on her own two feet and make her designs a success without using the Fiorini name to do it.

Small promises Mimi had made with every intention of keeping them.

At the time.

But it was so hard now that she was alone.

Her eyes closed and just for a second she gave into her desperate need to sit back in her chair and steal an hour or two of wonderful, refreshing sleep in the early-morning calm before the storm of the day ahead of her.

Working late was nothing new, but she had

become so desperate to make sure that her work was the very best it could be for this showcase that working until two or three in the morning had started to become the norm over the past few weeks since Poppy had agreed to stage the show.

Her designs were good—she knew that—but even in these last few days she was still looking for ways to improve. She could feel the strain of the pressure of continually altering and reshaping the garments, pushing herself harder than she had ever pushed herself before. There was so much work she could still do. It was not surprising that she felt so stretched out, beyond tired and pushed to the limit.

And so very much alone.

She envied Poppy so much; at least she had a brother who was willing to drop everything to come and help when she needed him.

Sniffing away the wave of sleep-deprived grief that threatened to overwhelm her, Mimi forced herself onto her feet with a sigh and drew open the full-length glazed patio doors which led to the flight of stairs linking her flat to the shop below, and the paved area which was both her delivery bay and what served as her small private garden.

Through this open door she looked out onto the gardens of the family homes on the other side of the small lane that separated the shops from the residential area around them.

She had been looking at the same view every morning for as long as she could remember.

Seasons were measured through the changes in the tall mature trees which towered over the lane from her neighbours' gardens: the fresh green leaves of beech and lime blossom in the spring; lilacs and apple blossom; a silver birch with its silvery leaves and shiny bark.

And her favourite: a mature cherry tree which had to be at least forty feet tall. Soft pink-and-white blossom had been replaced now with young cherries, much to the delight of the wild birds that spent much of their day in the tall branches.

These trees and gardens were such a part of her life now that she could not imagine eating breakfast without that view to enjoy. But the risk was very real. Without extra income she was in serious danger of losing the shop she had inherited from her parents, her chance of making a living and her home. The only home she had ever known—or ever wanted.

She had often wondered what it would be like to be a traveler, rootless and wandering, without a fixed place to call home.

Someone like Hal Langdon, for example.

Perhaps that was the reason he was so very, very fascinating. As a person, as a professional and very much as a man.

He was a mystery, a muscular, handsome, unshaven and challenging enigma. He was a man used to being completely spontaneous in his life and his work. Used to making decisions on the run.

But if anything that made her worry all the more.

Poppy knew her brother, and clearly must trust him well enough to leave him in charge of the charity project, but what if Hal had his own ideas for the show? Poppy Langdon had spent most of her working life either as a professional fashion model or in the trade. But what about her brother? All Mimi knew was that he was an adventurer, photographer and had once worked with Poppy when they were getting the events company off the ground—but that had been years ago.

Well, she would find out soon enough.

He had called late the previous evening to tell

her that Poppy had arrived safely in Florence and to arrange to meet at the studio the next morning to talk through the plans. She had explained that she would be at a student exhibition most of the day but that had not seemed to deter him in the least.

Mimi suddenly felt the need to sit down as the enormity of what she had taken on threatened to overwhelm her.

The last time she had trusted a photographer with her work had been at her first-ever photo shoot. He had been a well-known fashion photographer who had agreed to work with some of the top fashion-school graduates as part of a newspaper feature on new British talent. Her tutors adored him, the other students had sung his praises and she had been green enough to trust him with the theme for her graduation show. He'd even brought his own stylists.

It had been a complete and utter disaster, beginning to end. She had never been so humiliated in her life. Being laughed at and mocked was not fun. How did she know that Hal was not going to be the same? And now he had taken over from Poppy at

Langdon Events, which effectively meant that he was the boss—whether she liked it or not.

Yet she knew that she had no choice. She had committed to supplying the clothing; she had to go through with this.

It would be so wonderful to spend the whole weekend working on the show, but her normal salary paying life had to come first.

Saturday was the busiest day in the shop for the knitting classes she had started, so she had asked her friend Helena to help out in the shop and run the classes. Helena was one of her best customers and a natural saleswoman.

Apart from the shop, there were going to be six of her fashion-design students crammed into her studio for most of the morning—the ones who had left their hand-knitting course work to the very last minute—and they would all need help to complete their projects and get them to the gallery for their end-of-year exhibition before noon.

She exhaled loudly. The students needed to make the grades for their course work and it gave them a showcase for their work. She could not let them down now, especially when some of them had helped make the clothes for her collection.

And now Hal Langdon was going to turn up in person and add even more stress!

No pressure, then. None at all. *Whimper.*

She was exhilarated, exhausted and more excited than she had been for months.

Her mind kept wandering all by itself to Hal Langdon. The sexy way his amazing eyes creased around the edges as he smiled. That sensuous mouth.

It totally infuriated her that he had wormed his way into her brain like that.

It all went to prove one thing: she really should get out more!

But not now. Not when she was so close to achieving her dream.

Birdsong from the cherry trees rang out clear, sweet and invigorating through the open window and Mimi looked out into the faint sunshine and smiled.

In the same way that the trees broke out from their winter hibernation into fresh green buds of new growth, she needed to move forward to a new season in her life.

Poppy Landon might have given her a chance,

but now it was her turn to prove that she knew what she was doing.

She was going to show Hal Langdon that she was capable of handling any challenge that he could throw at her. They both wanted a great show and that was what they were going to create. She would listen; she would give her suggestions, help him understand how important elegance and sophistication were to her designs, and everything was going to be fine.

She was going to have to trust him. Because one thing was becoming so very clear: whether she was prepared to say it out loud or not, there were simply not enough hours in the day to do everything she needed to make this show a success. She needed Hal and Poppy even more than ever.

She had promised her mother that she would prove to the world that Mimi Ryan was as fine a designer as any other member of the Fiorini family.

But she was not just doing this for her mother. No. This was for *her*. She needed this boost to break her out of the past six months of painful grief and save her business.

Mimi turned to face a silver-framed photograph of a stunningly pretty dark-haired woman which was propped up by a cushion on the table, and raised her glass of orange juice in a toast.

'Happy birthday, Mum,' Mimi said. 'What do you think I should wear today? Any ideas?'

Hal Langdon steadied himself on his left crutch and raked the fingers of his right hand back over his scalp, pushing his hair away from his forehead. Maybe one of Poppy's stylist pals could give him a haircut after the show.

If they were not too exhausted by then.

He chuckled to himself at the thought of what he had just left behind in Poppy's apartment. His little sister had assembled a top team to make sure there would be enough models available for all of the clothing in Mimi's collection—namely her flatmates Lola and Fifi and their many friends who had agreed to give up a precious Saturday for a good cause.

This meant that his breakfast had been disturbed by an assortment of leggy fashion models bickering over yoghurt and cranberry juice while they planned their assault on the London shops in search of shoes, bags and luxury spa products—apparently all necessary preparation for a weekend of full-on pampering in advance of the big day.

Some men would have found being surrounded by gorgeous, leggy girls a sweet start to the day, but he had been through this process way too many times and the attraction had definitely worn off. There were only so many times you could tell a girl that her knees did not look fat in micro shorts—and the sound of excited females competing for attention while he was still in his boxers under a duvet on Poppy's sofa had been exhausting. Especially when they had decided to tease him about the new grey hairs on his chest, forcing him to decline the offer of both eyebrow tweezers and a free waxing-session.

They would enjoy seeing him suffer far too much.

Back in France, he had forgotten a few essential details about his sister's apartment—such as the fact that it was on the second floor and there was no lift. Oh, and that it only had two spare bed-rooms and that both of them were fully occupied by girls who managed to make the rooms feel even smaller. Hence his very uncomfortable night on the sofa with his leg propped up on the scatter cushions while he'd fought the urge to be outside under wide skies, all the while knowing that was not an option.

Cramped living space and several flights of stairs he could just about cope with. But he had not been prepared for the constant reminders of his life working with Tom Harris which had assailed his senses throughout the flat.

Tom Harris and Hal Langdon had made a name for themselves filming in the most dangerous and adrenaline-inducing locations on earth. Their photographs of the high mountains and the people who lived to climb them had been published in magazines and newspapers all over the world, vivid, sometime stark but always exciting and dramatic. They had won awards and prizes on every continent. And they had loved every second of it.

They had been champions of the universe, indestructible and fearless, destined to succeed at everything they set their mind to do. And they had succeeded time and time again.

The evidence of that success was captured in those photographs, which were everywhere he looked in Poppy's apartment.

She was so proud of her big brother and what he had achieved.

How could she know that now they only served as constant reminders that he had lost his best friend and probably his career at the same time? The doctors and specialists had made their prognosis quite clear—he had destroyed his ankle and broken his leg very badly. Even with ten surgical pins and two metal plates, the bones and supporting tendons and ligaments would never be the same again. His mountaineering days were over.

Every photograph and every image screamed out one message: *failure*. He had failed. Failed Tom, failed himself.

He had tossed and turned most of the night, and every time he had opened his eyes there was his best friend Tom grinning back at him from every wall, slim, rugged, happy and clever. A natural sportsman whose love of the high places and sense of humour had carried them through every hardship in supposedly inaccessible places photographers could not get to.

Their life had been a constant buzz of travel from one remote location to the next, until Tom had fallen in love with a supermodel who had brought him to his knees when she had returned his love. She'd even given up her career to show Tom what true happiness was like.

And then he had watched Tom die.

He was so angry with Tom. With himself. With the absurdity of life.

Lying on Poppy's sofa in the cool light of a London dawn, the constant reminders of his failure and his guilt threatened to overwhelm his determination to see his friend's legacy through to the end.

He had promised Poppy he would take care of the event and that was what he was going to do. Because if he didn't...? There was a limit to the number of failures a man could take in his life.

His little sister had been devious enough to call him back to work on a project she knew full well he would not be able to refuse. It had occurred to him several times as he'd tossed and turned that perhaps this emergency trip to Florence was just a little too convenient. Poppy had always adored working in Italy when she'd been a model. He suspected she had always planned to spend a few fun days with her friend in total indulgent luxury, finalising the no-doubt amazing wedding they had planned together. Leaving him to hold the fort.

Clever; very clever. She had lured him back to work in the full knowledge that once he had committed to the project he would not allow it to fail.

It dared not fail.

A shiver ran down his neck and across his shoulders. Hal shuffled inside his leather jacket and shifted his crutch to a new position so that he could massage his right thigh muscle which had started to cramp.

He swallowed down the rush of intense resentment, pain and regret that had overwhelmed him so many times these last few months that they were starting to feel like familiar friends. The kind of friends it would be too easy to welcome inside so that they could all wallow and feel sorry for each other and drown in the anguish of painful memories.

Pain kept him alert, alive. Even if it had robbed him of his sleep.

He had spent most of the night putting together an action plan based on the notes Poppy had left him. By the time the girls had taken control of the bathroom that morning, he had made deals for equipment and props which would make this a show to remember.

Providing, of course, that the clothing was as stylish as Poppy had suggested. She did have excellent taste, but all he had seen so far were sketches and a few photographs. Could Mimi Ryan deliver on time? He had been impressed with her energy yesterday. Time to find out more about Studio Designs and exactly how much of a challenge he had just taken on.

If he could find the place!

He stared across at a small row of shops then double-checked the address Poppy had given him. This was the right street, only there was no sign of a warehouse or stylish boutique of any type.

Hobbling across the quiet London road, Hal quickly scanned the numbers above each of the shops. There had to be a mistake because Studio Designs should be at this address instead of a knitting shop called Etalia Yarns.

Well, that couldn't be right.

Perhaps there was another street with the same name in another part of this area. London was a huge city; there was bound to be some duplication.

Or was it possible that Studio Designs was hidden away at the back of these shops?

It would make sense for him to enquire inside.

Hal sniffed, pulled his camera bag over his right shoulder and grasped his crutch more tightly as he stared at the front entrance of Etalia Yarns.

A knitting shop; this was going to be a new experience. Tom Harris had taught him to be an explorer and an observer in any new location, no matter where, and those skills still served him well. He liked the small things that told him a story about the people and the place.

It was the details he looked for as a photographer—the tiny body movement and individual characteristics that made one sportsman unique and could make or break an action photograph. It had become second nature for him to look for exactly those details in every shot.

Now he took the time to take a closer look at the shop itself—or rather what looked like a small house in a normal-looking street of family homes mixed with small shops: a dry cleaner, a hairdresser and Etalia Yarns.

The name had been etched out in a large cursive font along the top half of a large picture-window which would have been the bow window of the living room when this house had been a home. The bottom half was etched glass with a scrolling curling pattern.

The green-and-white paintwork was fresh and attractive. A large, circular brass door-knocker completed the look.

The only vaguely kitsch thing about the shop window was the tiny long-haired toy sheep which had been placed on the inside window-ledge so that it seemed to be looking out to face the street. A broad black smile in the shape of a half circle shone out in welcome.

So this was what an upmarket knitting-yarn shop looked like? He was clearly way out of date!

But where was Studio Designs?

The same minute that thought came into his head he spotted a small metal plaque which had been screwed into the door frame above his head: Studio Designs. At last!

Well, well. Mimi Ryan worked above, beyond or inside a knitting shop.

Who knew what strange new customs and traditions the inhabitants followed? He certainly had no clue what to expect.

Which was far more interesting and exciting—not that he would ever admit it—than he had expected.

Into the unknown.

Just as Hal shuffled forward towards the entrance, two teenage girls in denim trousers and bright T-shirts giggled their way past him and through the shop door, giving him sly glances as they did so. Each of them was carrying a bulging, oversized plastic bag and it made perfect sense for Hal to hold open the door and slip after them into the shop.

Or, rather, a gallery of rainbows.

Pale wooden storage-cubes were aligned along every available piece of wall space, and each cube was stuffed with yarn in a complete spectrum of rainbow colours from deepest purple through blues, greens and yellows, to reds and pinks and white and cream. It was as familiar to a photographer as his favourite camera. And it was twice as pleasurable to see the raw energy of colour softened by textures, shapes and sizes.

Natural light from two long windows filled the narrow space, helped by down-lighters of just the perfect intensity and spectrum to make the colours of the yarn pop in their display cubes.

Very clever.

Instead of stacks of yarn, the long narrow room had been split into two halves by a long antique pine dining-table with comfy chairs on each side. Two older women were selecting soft balls of tweedy stuff from wooden baskets piled high with yarn, while the teenagers laughed and giggled their way to the back of the room.

Their girlish laughter was shared with a tall woman with an amazing figure who was facing away from him, one arm around the shoulders of the youngest girl as they pulled out their creations from the plastic bags. He caught a glimpse of strands of yarn, what looked like string and a pair of enormous wooden knitting-needles that made his eyebrows lift.

Intrigued by the exhibits, and still in awe of the rainbow effect of the yarns around him, Hal slowly strolled down the room and smiled at the other customers, who seemed to be far too focused on the goods to pay him any attention. He was almost in the middle of the room when one of the teenagers spotted him and nudged the other, and the woman turned around to face him.

And every thought in his brain was frozen, mesmerised by the stunning woman he was looking at.

It was Mimi Ryan.

He should have recognised the hair, the creamy skin, the voluptuous figure which had only been hinted at in the street and later in Poppy's office.

Forget hinting; this version of Mimi was full-on gorgeous.

The black trousers fitted her so perfectly that they must have been made to measure, but it was her coral-coloured knitted top that burnt a pattern in his retinas.

The soft, flowing fabric looked to have faint, pink, fine stripes with a cleverly constructed narrow lapel, fitted in at the waist so that there was no mistake that this lady was curvy—and meant business.

Light from a stained-glass panel in a side window fell onto one side of Mimi's face highlighting her high cheekbones and delicate chin and features. The bow lips and warm smile seemed to illuminate her face as she turned around to face him and grinned.

With the coral top bringing a natural glow to her skin, Mimi Ryan was stunning.

If he was a receiver then Mimi Ryan was sending out just the right messages to flick on all of his switches. And it sent his brain into a spin.

Red warning-lights started flashing. This was the last thing he had been expecting and it shocked him to the core.

He could not allow himself to be attracted to a city girl like Mimi. Not now, not ever. He was *not* going down the same route that Tom had taken. He had to bury that telltale prickle of attraction as fast as possible.

This was probably why he found himself incapable of doing anything more than nodding when Mimi finished chatting to the girls and strolled over to him so that they were only inches apart.

Luckily for him, Mimi took the initiative and broke the tension he had not fully realised existed by speaking first. Her voice was light, warm and as welcoming as a faint breeze on a hot day. He revelled in the very sound of her voice.

She was captivating and he swallowed down a

tinge of regret and resignation that he would never see her as anything more than a girl he had to work with over the next week to get the job done.

It was a pity his body had not received that message yet.

'Good morning, Mr Langdon. I hope you slept well.' Mimi smiled. 'I wouldn't want to wear you out on your first day back.' Her mouth creased into a cheeky grin which was impossible to ignore.

Since speech was barely possible, he stretched out his right hand and wrapped his long fingers around hers. Her hand was soft, warm and surprisingly delicate, with fine bones, but she pulled away before he had a chance to decadently slide his fingers down the back of her hand.

'Oh, I think I can manage,' he stammered out and stood back to pretend to admire the room. 'And please call me Hal. Are you ready to go? I thought we might make an early start. Is Studio Designs upstairs?'

Mimi looked at him with raised eyebrows for a second before biting her lower lip.

'This *is* Studio Designs, Mr Langdon,' she replied. 'This is my knitting shop and my studio.' Lifting both arms in the air, Mimi gestured gracefully around the room. 'Welcome to my world.'

CHAPTER THREE

'I TOOK over the family knitting business about a year ago, but I also use the workshop area at the back of the shop for Studio Designs. That way I can move between the two projects any time I like, and so far it has worked extremely well.'

'A knitting shop. Wow,' he gushed, cursing himself for being so out of control of his faculties. 'Not that I have much experience of yarn stuff.'

In desperation, and anxious to find something to do with his hands, he snatched up a loose ball of what looked like thick fur, except that it was pink with a silver thread going through it.

'What do you make with this type?' Hal asked, turning to Mimi with the yarn still in his hand.

'I don't use that particular fashion yarn for my designs,' she replied, stroking an identical ball in a basket on the table. 'But the students love eyelash—the brighter and flashier the better. A bit of fun; it's great. And makes terrific scarves.'

Hal nodded and carefully replaced the ball very slowly onto the table. 'Eyelash. Scarves. Right.' He looked back to see Mimi smiling across at him.

It struck him powerfully that this was the first time he had seen Mimi smile from the heart. His photographer's sense of vision caught the telltale curvature of her lips and the gentle, warm creases at the corners of her shining eyes. Back in Poppy's office Mimi had seemed too stunned by the sudden change in management to be herself, but here it was different. Here she was in her own world and the difference was startling.

She should smile more often.

'This is the first time you've been into a shop like this, isn't it?' Mimi asked. 'That's okay. You don't have to be scared. The inhabitants are quite friendly most of the time—although I should probably warn you about a few local customs. Take yarn, for example.'

Mimi walked across to the next set of cubes and drew out a ball of a fine, smooth fibre in a deep red colour. As he watched, she unconsciously stroked the fibres as she squeezed the small ball, eyes half-closed, an almost sensual pleasure warming her face in the few seconds it took him to hobble the few steps to stand next to her.

'Squidging is an essential part of our daily rituals. This is one of my favourites: silk; fine-spun, twisted with viscose to increase the shine. Here, have a try. You'll soon get the hang it.' She held out the yarn to him, forcing him to look away from the smooth skin and amazing mouth.

It was not often that he was wrong about women, but he had been wrong to judge Mimi yesterday. The passion she had for these yarns shone out from her in the way she spoke and handled these bundles of thread with such loving care. She meant it. It could be that Mimi Ryan did know the fashion trade after all.

Her enthusiasm swept him along so much that he was taken aback by the tiny ball of soft stuff she held out towards him, and he made a point of rubbing a few strands between his finger and thumb. Her fingers were long with pale neat-polished nails. No rings.

In contrast, his fingers were rough and calloused and furrowed by deep ridges from holding ropes and cables and grappling for tiny hand-holds on rock faces where his life had depended on being able to take his weight on his fingers. His fingers and hands were as important as any other piece of equipment he relied on to keep him alive.

The rough skin instantly snagged on the delicate fibres and he released his grip. He had no business touching balls of the softest silk.

But he could still enjoy the sensation for a moment through what few nerves were left in his fingertips.

'How am I doing?'

'Not bad,' Mimi replied, stepping closer. 'Try stroking rather than squeezing the life out of it. That's better.'

'Nice colour. What can you make with it?'

He looked up into her face and made the mistake of focusing on her eyes. They were mostly green, and in those heels she was not much shorter than he was.

'Anything you like; that's the magic. You take this ball of thread and two sticks and out comes a fabric. The cardigan I'm wearing came from a blend just like this one.'

Mimi popped the cherry-coloured ball back into its slot and pointed to the next cube.

'You made it yourself?' Hal asked, genuinely impressed as he glanced down at the fitted coral top, which up close he could see had some sort of twisted design down one side.

'Please don't sound quite so surprised, Mr Langdon. I *am* a textile designer, and this is my work. And my pleasure. Does nobody in your family knit by hand?' Mimi asked. 'It's quite a tradition in mine.'

Hal chuckled out loud at that one, and the sound of his own merriment shocked him more than he cared to admit. It had been a while, months, since he had last felt like laughing. There had to be something in the air in this shop. Was it the colours, or the talented woman who had asked him a question?

He shook his head. 'I don't think so. Maybe Poppy made me a scarf once when we were at school, but I don't remember what happened to it. No; Poppy likes to shop, buy things other people have made—designed—whatever.' He paused for a few seconds as Mimi rearranged the balls into a neater design. 'I don't think a creative gene runs in our family. Not so far, anyway,' Hal added, well aware that he was babbling now and relieved that

Mimi did not seem to mind that he was acting like a loon and probably thought that he was trying to play the idiot.

If the cap fits...

'Um, well, that might be a problem,' Mimi murmured, just as a bustle of activity swept into the room on a wave of female laughter and bawdy bellows. 'I'll be right back. My Saturday knitting club has just arrived and the Knitty Chickies are on a mission.'

She gestured to a door at the back of the showroom which had been decorated with pictures of cute kittens playing with balls of yarn. 'Studio Designs is just through there. Why don't you have a look around for a few minutes? My college students are getting ready for their end-of-term exhibition but they won't be in your way. Please feel free to explore. You'll find a map and compass near the door on your way in.'

And with that Mimi was immediately swallowed up by the group of ladies of all ages who clustered around her like chicks around a mother hen and drew her into their conversation and laughter which echoed around the room.

Just as Hal opened the door to the studio, he took

one glance back to see what Mimi was doing. Her head was back and she was laughing out loud with the other ladies at some joke about knitted body parts. Her laughter came from deep inside her body, a resonating, sweet, joyous sound that was strangely distinctive, even though this was the first time he had heard it. Her voice was musical and warm—and something else. Something special. Something genuine. She was the real deal, and as unique a character as he had ever met anywhere in the world.

The Knitty Chickies were clearly enjoying knitting a lot more than he was, and the camaraderie of their group made his throat tighten.

Suddenly he felt very much alone.

This room and these women were all a very long way from the Alps, and the narrow ice-covered ridge where his life had changed for ever.

What was he doing here? Mimi Ryan must think he was totally pathetic—and she would be right!

His world was ice picks, crampons and cold-weather cameras—not knitting yarn or women's clothing. Not even close.

It was pathetic that he should think working on a fundraising event could in any way lessen the weight of the overwhelming blanket of guilt that hung heavy around his shoulders.

A week; he could give this project a week of his life. He owed it to Tom.

Then he would work on the small matter of what he was going to do with the rest of his life.

Suddenly Hal was not so sure he could handle any more surprises in one day. Turning reluctantly away from the life, energy and joy in the knitting shop, he hobbled into Mimi's studio and closed the door behind him.

He stood in silence for a few seconds to take in the room.

In contrast to the kaleidoscope-shock of textures and colours in the shop area, the studio walls and woodwork had been painted in a pale cream which seemed to absorb the overhead light and reflect it back onto four large worktables which took up over half the floor space.

This was quite an achievement. The studio was the width of the entire shop building, and at least thirty feet long.

The overall effect was stunning and professional.

One thing was clear: this was a work room, not a hobby store.

From the hard-sealed flooring to the false ceil-ing-panels, it was the kind of spotless clean space which made Hal want to whisper and take off his boots—then run riot with a paintball gun just for the fun of it. As it was, his crutch hammered out his presence with every step.

A group of teenage girls were busy at the far end of the room, which was flooded with natural light from what looked like patio doors, so he strolled up to the nearest long white table. It seemed to be covered with all shapes, sizes and colours of amazing objects.

He bent over slightly and squinted at the printed labels on cards folded in front of each object: 'knit-ted installations'.

On the far left was a cheerful and completely realistic tea set: knitted cups with handles, knitted saucers, plates, sugar bowl and even a milk jug. On the plate were knitted cakes with knitted coils of white toppings made from a thicker white yarn. Everything was in bright primary colours—perfect for kids. The label on the solid maple-wood tea tray said: 'soft tea'.

The next table was 'wearable art' and there was only one exhibit—but it was certainly different. A short sleeveless tube of knitted mesh shaped like a dress was hanging on a tailor's-model form. It seemed to be made of coated electrical cable, and two wires were hanging from the dress, one on each side. The left was attached to what looked like a normal old-style cassette player. The other was wired into the back of a large amplifier.

Okay. He took a breath before checking the label a little more carefully this time: 'because your clothing says something about you. Press Play on the tape to hear about who's wearing the dress. Rewind when you leave. Thanks'.

'Hello again. Found anything you like?'

Hal turned around so that he could face Mimi as she walked up next to him and scanned the studio, turning his head from side to side.

'You weren't kidding about the student work. Is this the last group of exhibits?'

Mimi nodded. 'Yep. The college transport-system is a little slow today. In the meantime, feel free to wander around and take a look. You are welcome to come with me to the gallery if you like. I only need to be there for a few hours this morning and we can talk on the way.'

'Okay. That sounds like a plan.' Hal nodded and

glanced around. 'This is actually a very impressive studio. Has this always been a knitting shop?' he asked as Mimi stood next to him, gently packing away loose hanks of chocolate-and-cream yarn into long, transparent plastic boxes.

'A gentleman's tailor. My father trained with Mr Bloom for years before he decided to go into the wholesale business, but he loved working here. So, when the house and workshop came onto the market, my mother made the old maestro an offer he couldn't refuse. He's retired now, but he only lives a couple of streets away and comes in now and again. The skylights and patio were his idea, and they still work. You need natural light for colour matching.'

Mimi stopped packing and looked at Hal with a shrug. 'Sorry; I was forgetting you are a photographer. You probably know a lot more about light than I do. Please carry on.'

'What do you use the tables for?' Hal asked, blushing slightly at her compliment, and gestured at the huge long smooth surfaces stretching the width of the room.

Mimi paused for a second and took a breath. 'I am a designer, Mr Langdon,' she sighed, then looked at him in surprise. 'This is where I assemble the finished garments, collate together the knitting kits I sell on the Internet and cut out fabric patterns. Oh, and I run workshops for college students three days a week. I am so lucky to have this space. Good studios are very hard to find in this part of London.'

'Tell me about it,' Hal replied with a snort of exasperation. 'I am going to have to find somewhere to work and set up a centre of operations for the show before Monday or I am toast.'

'What about Poppy's office in Covent Garden?' Mimi asked, her brows coming together in concern. 'Or the hotel where we are staging the event? Don't they have spare rooms you could use?'

'Poppy's office is already cramped enough without trying to pack technical equipment into it. Besides, I don't do well in cramped offices.' Hal pursed his lips and shrugged his shoulders as he frowned. 'As for the hotel? I called in to introduce myself this morning. They did have two reception rooms we could have used, but the plans have changed. They are renovating the upper floors ahead of schedule and they need those rooms for storage. Poppy persuaded the manager to give us the ballroom, but I think we are lucky to have it—all of which leaves me looking for some space to rent in a hurry.'

She tilted her head slightly before asking in a deliberately sweet and angelic voice, 'Really? So you will need to rent some studio space? For *my* catwalk show?'

'Absolutely, and…' Hal paused and clasped his free hand around the back of one of the work chairs to take the weight from his ankle as the implication of what she was saying hit home. 'Unless, of course, you happen to know of a studio around here that might have some spare capacity? *Mimi*?'

Mimi pressed a forefinger to her chin and tapped a couple of times while looking at the ceiling for inspiration. 'Well. I might be able to find some studio space that Langdon Events could rent, *Hal*. At a very reasonable rate, of course, seeing as the project is for charity. And seeing as I will be directing my own stage show from here. I suppose it makes sense for you to pop in now and then and report back to Poppy on how I am getting on.'

Hal clenched the back of the chair a little harder.

'Don't you mean that it might be easier for you to pop in from the knitting shop to see how I am making progress with the design for your catwalk? Langdon Events is still in charge of the fundraising event.'

'Agreed. You have responsibility for the venue and promotion and the like, but when it comes to my launch show I really do need to be involved in the decision-making process. As far as I am concerned, you are here today so you can pick up a few tips on how it should be done. So that if—and it is a big if—I have a few small jobs that I need help with you might have some idea about how to go about it. That sounds much better.'

Hal snorted out loud at her reply, but when he looked up at her she was smiling.

'Here is a suggestion: this show is important to both of us. I need to raise as much cash as I can for the Tom Harris Foundation, and you need the media to rave about your clothing designs so the world can see how talented you are. Right? Right. It seems to me to point one way.'

'Oh?' Mimi asked. 'And what way is that?'

'We both want what is best for this show, and at the moment it looks like Poppy won't be back until later in the week, which means that we are on our own. For better or worse, we need to work together.

I need space, you have the space. Langdon Events will pay the going commercial rate and we can focus on what is really important—making the show the best that it can be.'

He paused just long enough for the impact of what he was suggesting to hit home, then gave her a full-on, maximum-strength grin complete with dimples and white, white teeth that would have defrosted a frozen dinner in ten seconds flat.

'What do you say? Truce, partner?'

Mimi pulled back slightly so as not to get burned by the charm offensive designed to melt the coldest of hearts, and cursed herself for being practical enough to want the rental fee while being able to keep tight control over the arrangements for the show.

The fact that Hal Langdon came with the deal was just something she was going to have to deal with. At least they were getting to know each other a bit better now.

Unfortunately he also had a good point—like it or not, they were on their own and would have to combine talents to make this project work.

He was certainly right about one thing—they both needed this show to be a huge success.

Mimi breathed in slowly and calmed herself. A few hours a day; that was all he was talking about. And it meant that she could be directly involved in any decisions that needed to be taken without having to leave her shop to travel to Covent Garden every day for the next week.

Which is why she squeezed her lips together and nodded. 'Okay. Truce it is. You can rent the space for the next week at the going rate, on condition that we really do work together on this show and you include me in any decisions. Do we have a deal?'

Yes! Hal felt like punching the air. At last he had finally managed to score a point with this girl and find a space large enough with high enough ceilings so that he did not feel the walls were pressing in on him. The hospital had warned him about cabin fever but he had never expected borderline claustrophobia. Poppy's office was so small he felt stifled.

This room was going to make a huge difference.

The morning was turning out a lot better than he had expected.

He could not resist rubbing his palms together

and giving Mimi a sharp nod. 'Excellent. How soon can I get started?'

Mimi lowered her hands and got back to the task of packing yarn for the exhibition for a few seconds to allow her offer to sink in before going on.

'Once these exhibits are cleared, I will be working flat out to get the fashion collection ready for the show. The patio leads onto the rear yard, so you would be free to come and go as you want.'

Hal scanned the room from side to side before nodding slowly several times. 'This is good. This is going to work; I like it. What about the computer side—Internet, that sort of thing?'

'Right here.'

Tucked into a corner of the room was an L-shaped modern polymer desk with a top-of-the-range desktop computer connected to a pair of large flat-screen monitors and a modern tower processing-unit. The scanner and printer were arranged in a straight line to the right of the keyboard and digital drawing tablet. It was neat, clean, organized, impressive. A large artist's portfolio-case covered most of the side table, which was supported by a cabinet fitted with wide shallow map-drawers.

Mimi gestured to the keyboard. 'I do most of my design work directly on-screen. Please take a seat.'

'Thank you,' he said, taken aback about the order and calm of the work station. 'Why don't you just start up like normal, and I'll ask questions as we go?'

Mimi dropped into a hard, wooden dining-room chair, which looked like something his sister would have thrown out twenty years earlier, and pointed to a matching chair a few feet away. It was fitted with a tapestry cushion embroidered with pink-and-white rabbits with the word 'Bunnies' in brown across the top. 'Please sit. You must need to rest your leg by now.'

'Thank you,' he murmured and half collapsed onto the wide carver chair. The relief was so great that he had to fight off the urge to sigh out loud. By kneading his thigh muscles hard with both fists, the aching pain and pressure of his weight on the smashed bones in his ankle was almost bearable. The last few days had been too much too soon and his bones were certainly complaining today.

It was only when he opened his eyes and looked

up that he had realised that Mimi was already working hard on her computer.

'You've taken your shoes off,' Hal murmured out loud, and was instantly embarrassed. He had not intended to draw attention to the fact that he was staring at Mimi's feet. They were wrapped in thin black stockings and she wrapped them around the back legs of the chair in a totally sensual way so that the soles of her feet were pitched towards him. A wave of heat made him sit back in the damned uncomfortable chair. What was it about this woman? *Get a grip, man.*

'Must be a bit cold,' he said in an over-loud voice, trying to sound as casual and unconcerned as possible. 'Without shoes, I mean.'

Mimi pulled her legs forward, looked down at her feet and grinned. 'Force of habit. I didn't even realise I had done that but, no, I'm never cold in here. Usually way too busy, even when I am tired.'

'Tired?'

Mimi nodded but did not turn around as she logged on to the computer and opened up the broadband Internet connection.

'If you recall, we did work quite hard yesterday before Poppy had to take off. And there is always work to do on the collection. You'll be pleased to know that I actually finished the hand sewing on the last two evening dresses yesterday, and the others should be ready in time.'

His smile faltered. 'Yesterday? I don't want to be critical, but isn't that leaving it a little late when the show is less than a week away?'

Mimi chuckled. 'Not at all. I can think of two professional fashion shows where the clothes were being finished in the changing room ten minutes before the models had to wear them on stage. In my case the crystals I ordered did not arrive until late last month. The original supplier sent the wrong colour, and I had to send them back, so that really delayed things.'

He squeezed his eyebrows together before replying. 'Crystals come in more than one colour?'

She sniffed once and shook her head slowly from side to side.

'You see, this is where specialist technical knowledge is so important. Although I suppose it does mean that there is one small job which you could help me with.'

'Ouch!' The killer smile flashed back on and

Mimi positively basked in the heat of it. 'What do you need me to do?'

Without a second's hesitation, Mimi turned fully towards him and leapt in with a smile. 'The two evening gowns have to be photographed for the show catalogue. Poppy was waiting for these last two dresses to be finished before organising the photographer and models. Do you think you could organise that in her place? Or would you like me to arrange it? That way you could just give me the job of catwalk director now and save time. You could just go home now and leave me to it.'

Hal chuckled out loud, the deep-belly sound echoing around the studio, and the teenagers went silent for a second then started giggling again at the back of the room.

'Oh, I think I can manage that, Miss Ryan. Besides, I would hate to miss the student exhibition. How could you be so cruel as to suggest such a thing? I have been looking forward to it all morning!'

'Oh, you wouldn't have to miss it at all,' she replied in a flash. 'Everyone is welcome. So, you see, you could let me arrange things, rent the studio and see the exhibition—and all in one morning. Now, doesn't that sound efficient? Or are you scared of taking the risk now you are trapped inside unfamiliar territory?'

CHAPTER FOUR

HAL rocked back on the hard wooden chair so hard that he had to clutch on to the edge of the desk to stop himself from tipping the chair backwards.

Scared of taking a risk? Ridiculous.

The challenge knocked him sideways. A swell of focused energy bubbled up from deep within him, shocking him with its intensity. This show was *his* responsibility. He was accountable to Poppy and to Tom.

But for the first time since Poppy had passed over the reins he started to feel excited and even invigorated by the task he had been given. Perhaps this *was* the ideal project to shake him out of his grief and give him a reason to get out of bed in the morning.

One thing was already clear—he was going to need Mimi Ryan to make it a success. But how?

'You are not going to let this drop, are you?' Hal asked.

'Nope. I shall persist until you realise that I am the best and only person to manage the show. Resistance is futile.'

'Well, that remains to be seen,' he eventually managed to say, then nodded to the PC. 'Thanks for showing me the computer. Have we got time to see the rest of the studio before heading out?'

Mimi stretched sideways to look over Hal's shoulder to check what the girls were doing, and nodded as she gathered her papers together. 'At least another five minutes. Right this way, just past the knitting kits and pattern books.'

Hal was just about to speak when he pointed at the bundle of pink and lavender cards on Mimi's desk. 'Are those your birthday cards?'

Mimi picked up a bright pink card with a picture of a cat wearing a tutu on the cover. 'You are very observant. Yes, they are birthday cards. But these are for my mother, not for me.'

Mimi popped the cards into her bag so quickly that Hal did not have a chance to look at them, and she started walking down the room. 'The bathroom and shower are just down to the right and there is a refrigerator next to the big table. We have a kettle and toaster, so you could call it a mini-kitchen, if you like.'

'Hey, slow down,' he replied, having decided to ignore the fact that she wanted to change the subject as soon as she possibly could. 'Tell me more about the refrigerator—my guys like their beer.'

Mimi's pace slowed and she glanced at him before asking, 'Exactly how many guys are you talking about? I don't want a complete invasion.'

'Two on lighting and sound and at least three or four at the event, so more than a couple of volunteers would be here at any one time.'

'Oh, that's fine,' she breathed with a sigh of relief. 'These tables are designed to seat eight but I can squeeze in a full class of fourteen at a push.'

Hal nodded. 'Ever thought of going into sales? Oh, wait—' he smiled '—you are in sales.'

Mimi narrowed her eyes in reply. 'Anything else I can show you, Mr Langdon?'

'What do you use that space there for?'

Hal pointed to a fine mesh screen which had been decorated with découpage flowers of old roses and summer flowers.

'A room divider,' she replied a little too quickly and Hal's brow pulled together.

Oh, no; she had completely forgotten about the screen and the single bed!

When her mother had been ill, she had not been able to manage the stairs, and Mimi had set up a bed for her in the studio where she could see the patio garden and be close to the bathroom and work area at the same time. That way Mimi could chat and keep an eye on her during the day. The vascular dementia that had followed her mother's first stroke was a side effect they had not been prepared for—and when the confusion and distress became too great it had been reassuring for her mother to be in the same room as Mimi.

Of course, she had not been able to bring students here during those terrible months, but it had been worth it for the extra time that they had shared together.

Mimi turned away from Hal and lifted back the screen against the wall. Her fingers stroked the pink full-blown roses that they had stuck onto the mesh together in an effort to create some privacy when she had wanted to sleep or, at the end, weep.

Mental illness was so cruel, especially when it

happened so quickly. One day her mother had been a normal, happy woman, and the next…

She closed her eyes and swallowed down a surge of regret and grief. Perhaps this was all happening too soon; she wasn't ready for the upset and turmoil in her life. Not yet. Not when she was so very, very tired.

One example of the turmoil was right at her side.

'If it is all the same to you I think I will turn the screen around. Too girly! But the bed is just fine.'

'Yes, you are probably right,' she quickly replied, gathering herself together and plastering on a smile, but not daring to look him in the face quite just yet. Instead she bustled forward and was just opening one of the long double-glazed doors when her brain registered what Hal had just said.

'I'm sorry. Did you say that the bed is just fine?'

'Sure. Normally I would bring my tent and camping gear but sleeping in a tent would be a little tricky at the moment.'

Hal knocked his crutch twice against the floor and leant on it a little heavier than normal for dramatic effect. 'Have you been to my sister's apartment? Two flights of stairs. No lift. It took me ten minutes to make it down this morning. I need somewhere to stay, and this would be ideal, all on the ground floor and fully equipped. I'll have no problem sleeping down here.'

Sleeping here? When had she agreed to that?

'Wouldn't you be better off in a hotel or a bed and breakfast?'

Hal scrubbed the back of his head and thought about just how much he was prepared to share with Mimi, who was looking at him with such surprise and alarm in her eyes that there was only one thing to do—trust her with just enough about himself to seal the deal.

'The truth is I have spent most of the last five months either in hospital or in a wheelchair, trapped indoors. A prisoner in my own home. I never realised how many stairs there were in my chalet until I had to negotiate them every day just to reach the bathroom or kitchen. After a few months, it really does feel like the walls are closing in on you.'

He gestured with one hand to the sunlit patio on the other side of the glass doors. 'I adore Poppy, but her apartment and her office are too small and congested for me right now. Same goes for London hotels. Sorry, I am not explaining myself very well—but I need the high ceilings and air to breathe. Does that make any kind of sense?'

Mimi leant back against the edge of the table so that she was facing Hal when she replied, but she made him wait several full seconds which seemed to go on for ever before giving her answer. 'Actually, it makes perfect sense. I can see that you would have problems with the stairs, and a cramped London flat is hardly what you are used to. Although, I should warn you, it can get pretty busy around here.' She lifted her chin a little higher and caught the full force of him in switched-on, testosterone-seduction mode.

His voice was an octave lower, and as he leant on the counter she could see the texture of his tongue as he licked his upper lip before talking. Her heart thumped in her chest.

He patted his shoulder bag and winked at her. 'Like you say, I am deep in foreign territory. I have my camping gear, my faithful camera at the ready and a couple of spare memory cards. I'm ready for anything.'

'And here we have the signature item of wearable art from today's show which I understand was designed by the course tutor for the students to work on. The label simply says "jacket of hand-knitted silk lace with embroidered silk moiré". And how exactly would you describe this piece, Miss Ryan? I'm sure our readers would be interested in your design concept.'

Mimi smiled patiently at the fashion reporter from a major London newspaper who had arrived only minutes after the student exhibition had opened.

'I would be happy to, Paul. As you can see, the shape of the jacket was inspired by classical Japanese haori clothing. Studio Designs specialises in fine hand-knitting, so my idea was to create a three-dimensional effect by adding a layer of hand-knitted lace over an embroidered silk jacket in a contrast colour. The lining is moiré silk, with the same flowers embroidered in silver. Each layer of the jacket was completed by a separate team of students, so this truly is a masterpiece made by all of the students here today.'

The words had barely left Mimi's lips when Hal Langdon came in through the main entrance to the student exhibition and stood, frozen, directly in front of the jacket as the breeze from the door gently separated the delicate thin layers of knitted lace so that the silk fabric shone through in shimmering, iridescent blue and green shades.

To Mimi's delight there was a spontaneous round of applause and sighs of rapture from the students. Mimi left Paul taking photographs and chatting to the students and strolled over to Hal.

'Do you like it?' Mimi asked Hal, not sure what his reply was going to be, judging from the stunned look on his face.

This was one part of showing her work that she always dreaded at student shows—the judging. Whether it was the professional tutors who would award the students their marks, or family or guests, it was still her original design that the students had worked on and she never got used to the whirls of anxiety which twirled around the pit of her stomach.

Mimi felt the heat rise on the back of her neck in tune with her blood pressure.

Of course, there was no way that Hal could know she had been fighting to escape her Fiorini design heritage all of her working life.

At college some of her fellow students had blatantly accused her of using Fiorini designs from decades earlier. Her tutors were constantly challenging her to be as different and controversial as possible to prove that she was capable of doing more than simply copying the ideas her mother had brought from Italy. Some had even asked her to arrange for them to work in Milan, assuming that she was part of the Fiorini family, with the influence to match.

If only they knew the truth!

It had taken years of working harder than anyone else on the course to convince her tutors that she was sincere about her determination to create her own style in her own way, without the support of a major couture design-house like Fiorini.

Even now, every time she made something, there was always the constant doubt that there could be something similar in the Fiorini archive. Her life seemed to revolve around constant checking of old catalogues to make sure she could never be accused of plagiarism, but it was so very difficult and so tiring to be constantly trying to defend her originality.

Hal knew nothing about her past or her connection to the famous family of couture designers. In fact, he did not know any more about her than she knew about him—which was precious little.

Which meant that his opinion was going to be totally unbiased, plain and direct.

She had made so much effort to help Hal Langdon understand her work and why her designs were so important to her she would hate it if he made some dismissive remark now, especially when the students had worked hard on the pieces. She needed him to like her designs and want to make them shine if they were going to work together over the next week.

Hal stepped slowly around the jacket one shuffling step at a time until he had made a full circle back to Mimi.

Mimi sidled up next to Hal and moved her head from side to side so that she could see the jacket from the same angles, only with her arms folded across her chest.

'Formed an opinion yet?' she asked impatiently, unable to disguise the frustration in her voice. 'You will notice that you could easily wear this jacket in the evening or during the day. And it is designed to fit the average-sized woman as well as the skinnier ones.'

'I'm getting there; keep your frillies on. It's just taking me a while. I do have a question that will help me make up my mind, if that's okay?' His head lifted and he glanced at her, waiting for her approval. Mimi unfolded her arms and flung open her fingers.

'Please.'

'You told the reporter that it was based on a Japanese design. Have you ever been to Japan to study the culture and art forms? Seen one like this?'

Mimi fought not to sigh out loud. Of course, she would have loved to study in Japan, but it had been totally out of the question. How could she confess to an experienced traveller like Hal that her world was so small and confined without totally humiliating herself even more? She would sound totally pathetic. Better to just tell him the truth and get it over with.

'I wasn't that lucky. The only time I have been out of London was a summer spent in Milan when I was 14. I didn't like it so I decided not to bother again. All my research has been through local museums, books and the Internet.'

Hal's mouth opened and his eyes widened. 'One trip to Milan,' he said incredulously. 'Wow.'

Then his shoulders straightened and he gave her a short bow from the waist, or as much of a bow as he could manage with his crutch. 'In that case, Miss Ryan, I am doubly impressed. I lived in Japan for a few months and I couldn't have captured the spirit of the clothing design as well as you have right here today. Congratulations. I am now officially impressed.'

And with one final flourish he twirled his right hand in the air with a twist and winked at her.

Mimi stared at him, open-mouthed, dumbfounded.

It was the very last thing she had expected Hal to say, and much to her horror she knew that she was flushing bright red at the base of her neck. Her throat suddenly seemed so tight she could not swallow.

He liked it. *He really liked it.* If she could have given out awards at that moment for making a girl feel better about herself, then Hal would have stood up with several laurel wreaths festooned around his unkempt hair and gold medals weighing heavily against that broad chest.

Now, how did she respond to that?

'Well, thank you. You are very kind.'

'Speak it as I see it,' he replied in a nonchalant casual voice and turned on his crutch to face the jacket. 'Only, could you do me a favour?' He twisted his head around to her and smiled. 'Please do not show my sister this jacket unless you have a stockpile ready to pull out at a moment's notice. I would never hear the end it if she found out I had seen an exclusive one-off and did not snap it up before anyone else had the chance. I don't suppose…?'

His eyebrows raised in a question, breaking the tension and really making her smile. 'Not mine to sell. This jacket was made by the students, and the hand-knitting alone took a week. So, no; no stockpile. But I might make her one as a present over the winter. How about that?'

Hal answered in a twist of his lips which was so charming and sweet that she could hardly contain her smile.

How did he do it? How did he manage to turn the subject around and make her feel less anxious without knowing a thing about her problems?

The expression on his face was so beguiling that

they stood entranced for a few seconds in silence, simply looking at one another, before a bustle of bright chatter and activity from the entrance snapped Mimi out of her reverie.

'If you would like to know more, the original concept-boards are right over here,' Mimi suddenly added in a louder voice before Hal had a chance to reply. She smiled warmly to the new visitors to the gallery as she walked over to a large display-panel covered with coloured drawings, fabric samples and photographs.

'Here are photographs of the actual jacket on display taken at various stages, right next to some pictures of the vintage jackets from London textile museums. The students have captured the natural elegance of the original design. Don't you agree?'

Hal hopped over to the photos she had taken in her studio and looked at each one in turn for several seconds, before nodding wisely and speaking in a normal voice against the background noise.

'Oh, yes. Completely agree.' He inched closer to Mimi and pretended to peer at the original sketch, before going on in such a soft voice that only Mimi would be able to hear him.

'Well, you said earlier that you were a fashion designer, and so you are.'

He lifted his head and turned so that their faces were only inches apart.

'Gotta love a talented woman,' he murmured, his voice low in his throat, before a soft smile widened his mouth and his brows came together. 'How about some outrageous flattery for the benefit of the students, seeing as I am now their greatest fan?'

He turned back to face the jacket and gave an exaggerated sigh of delight.

He fluttered his eyes at her outrageously and pretended to be awestruck as he suppressed a smile, but his eyes gave him away. The smile lines creased down over his cheeks and his whole face lit up.

Oh, no, she groaned inside. *Is that a dimple? Could he be more obvious—and attractive? Keep it together, keep it together.*

'That is the most wonderful piece of clothing any designer could ever have imagined. And so beautifully knitted. And sewn. And stuff. And it is the most brilliant and stunning thing in the room.' He lowered his voice and spoke out of the side of his mouth as Mimi stood next to him. *'Apart from us, of course.* How am I doing? Is that better?'

'Some slight improvement.' With that Mimi turned to face him and tilted her head to one side. 'So. You have seen my work, you have checked that I am capable of organising a student exhibition and along the way demonstrated that we seem to share the same excellent taste in jackets. Is there something else I need to do before you can trust me and listen to my ideas?'

What did Mimi have to do before he could trust her?

That simple question knocked the wind from his sails so effectively that he had to take a second before nodding a reply, reaching into his bag and drawing out his favourite digital camera. 'No promises. How about I take a few pictures and let you get on with your work? We can talk later.'

'Be my guest. The students will love it—as long as you don't take my picture, of course. I would hate to be responsible for breaking your camera. Today is all about the students, not me.' And with one final smile she turned back to the cluster of people who had just wandered into the room, chatting happily as Hal stood in stunned silence.

So, Mimi didn't want her photograph taken.

What was that all about?

By force of instinct, Hal turned on his light-weight digital camera and brought it up with his right hand, hiding most of his face behind the camera as he focused on the jacket that Mimi had designed, as it moved and lifted with the breeze from the entrance and the air-conditioning fans. He would take the time to capture its spirit as best he could—and wonder in awe how a girl from a knitting shop who'd barely left London had created something so exotic and beautiful.

The coordination between his hand and his eyes was so automatic that he did not have to concentrate on the how—only the subjects he wanted to capture and where.

He had never been interested in static objects and fixed diagrams—he wanted people. Especially people in action—how they walked, spoke, their mannerisms. People fighting the elements, or working with them to push themselves harder. That was what he was interested in.

The rest of the gallery was starting to fill up now with the friends and family of the students who were exhibiting, plus the local press and college newspapers. The room was bustling with activity and happy chatter. It was unlike any other exhibition gallery he had ever been to—which, to be fair, was not many, but they had always been stuffy and formal. In total contrast, the atmosphere of this exhibition was casual and unpretentious.

The knitting exhibits were displayed on round tables in clusters around the room so that the student could walk around each piece and chat about it from all sides. The overall atmosphere was unfussy, friendly, open and accessible. A delight. The space was probably an old college building transformed for the day into an exhibition space—and Mimi had done a terrific job. The lighting was soft, the walls were covered in just the right shade of cream to create a warm ambience for the textiles and the pedestals for the exhibits were just the right height. And, best of all, there were signs everywhere telling visitors that they could touch, feel and ask questions.

He liked it. He liked it *a lot*.

And if Mimi did not like having a photograph taken, well, he could work around that. Like now, for example. She had turned away from him to chat to a student, who looked so like the man and woman smiling next to her that they just had to be her proud parents.

Hal leant back against the wall and took several general shots of the area before subtly and slowly zooming in on Mimi. Her head was tilted slightly towards the student, so that her long neck was in profile. Strands of her auburn hair fell loosely onto the neck of her jacket, where the coral shade highlighted her creamy skin and delicate shoulders and arms.

One of her arms was resting on the exhibit table. The table held the knitted tea set he had seen in her studio, only now as he refocused the camera he could see that real cupcakes with soft, swirly icing piled on top had been added next to the knitted ones. A silver teaspoon was on the saucer. Sugar cubes were in the knitted sugar-bowl.

It was fun, it was unique and it made the work look ten times more appealing. The knitting itself had not changed, only the way it had been staged.

He hated that Poppy had been right when she'd told him that Mimi was perfect for the show. If this was an example of Mimi's work, then he could use someone who had that level of creativity.

His lens focused on her hand and the details of

her pale skin and short, unpainted nails. There was no vanity here; they were clever working hands she needed to create her work. He could see the way her fingers stroked the texture of the stitches on the knitted plate as she laughed with the parents, the way she moved her neck when she answered one of their questions. She was totally engrossed, giving the family her total attention, oblivious to the fact that she was the subject of his attention.

She was good with people and they warmed to her, sensing that she was genuinely interested in them and their work and had a passion for the craft.

She was like a butterfly in a desert, unique and special even when surrounded by colour, movement and light.

He had always admired butterflies, insects which by the rules of physics should not be able to fly or enchant but which achieved both in spectacular fashion. Rule breakers.

Every aspect of her body and movement became hyper-important and he followed her to the next exhibit, capturing her head and the side of her face and movements as she laughed, hugged and chatted with the crowd.

His finger pressed down on the shutter button

again and again until she was swallowed up by a cluster of people who were all clamouring for her attention and he lost her.

Hal lowered his arms.

What did Mimi have to do before he could trust her?

Wrong question. From that terrible day on the mountain, when Tom Harris had given him one last smile then stepped back to his death, there had only ever been one question.

How could he ever forgive himself for failing to save Tom's life?

That terrible failure meant that he was destined to carry the secret behind Tom's death to his own grave, if need be.

He could not share that burden with anyone. Not even his own sister—and especially not Tom's girlfriend, Aurelia, the beautiful woman Tom had sacrificed his own life to protect from the pain of having to watch him die from terminal illness.

What would Mimi Ryan say if she knew that he was the biggest fool in the universe? He had become expert at kidding other people that he had it in the bag, that he knew what he was doing, that he had it all worked out. When all the time he was hiding his guilt and the true extent of his loss from the world. After a lifetime of being an over-achiever, he had failed the one time it had truly mattered.

Would this beautiful, talented, warm, funny and authentic woman still want to work with him then?

CHAPTER FIVE

Two hours later Mimi followed Hal out of the gallery, and fell into step beside him.

'You know, you really were quite shameless in there! Fancy charming the head of the department with vague promises of a talk on textiles in the Andes in exchange for promotion of our fashion show on the college website! Devious. That is the word—*devious*. I had no idea that you took such an interest in traditional handicrafts,' Mimi said, dodging a cyclist.

He huffed at that. 'I must have hundreds of shots of local ladies knitting sweaters in the Andes. Might as well put them to good use.'

Mimi shot him a quick glance, not entirely sure that he was being serious. 'Um, and I look forward to seeing them. Do you normally resort to those sorts of devious practices in the name of publicity?'

'Oh, you would be surprised at the tricks I have up my sleeve. A lot of athletes would rather go to the dentist than have their photo taken. Paragliding? No problem. But put them in front of a camera, different story. Now, fashion models on the other hand? Ah. It is amazing how one sniff of pizza can motivate a girl—or a guy, for that matter.'

'Actually, I like my dentist, but I see your point,' Mimi said, checking the side roads for kamikaze motorcycles. 'You do know that I shall have to cross the street every time I see the poor woman? Just in case she asks me when you are coming back to give your talk.'

'Oh, ye of little faith. I will do it. Poppy will put something in my diary then chase me up at regular intervals to make sure that it happens. You can stay on the same side of the street in safety.'

'I am glad to hear it. Getting back to Langdon Events; is there much pressure—from Poppy, I mean—to follow in her proud footsteps and work on the management side? She does seem a little stressed at the moment.'

Hal sighed. 'I have been begging her to take an assistant ever since she took over the business on her own, but she is as stubborn as I am. Somewhere in her heart I think she still wants to go back to fashion modelling one day. In the meantime she's doing okay. Apparently she actually likes trying to pull together people, places, entertainment and the like, so that other people have fun. Enjoys it, even. That's why she leaves me to work on the sports and photography side of the business.'

Mimi negotiated two taxis and a bus before checking that Hal was still with her.

'Right!' Mimi rolled her eyes. Hal Langdon was so laid back he was practically horizontal. She could have thumped him, but instead she slipped past him and strolled into her shop, where her friend Helena was chatting happily to two regulars. As she indicated for Hal to go ahead into the studio, it was only too obvious that Helena had already been spreading the word about Mimi's new friend.

Even Mrs Papadopoulos—seventy-two, widow, twelve grandchildren, riddled with arthritis, always bought machine-washable acrylic—was checking out Hal's spectacular rear as he walked through.

Incredible.

Not that she blamed her. Those jeans could not have been tighter.

'Happy Birthday to Talia, my dear. Happy Birthday.'

'Thank you. You are very kind.'

Hal had already slipped off his jacket and was unpacking his camera bag by the time Mimi caught up with him at the computer desk. He gestured towards the stack of pink-and-purple envelopes while she tried not to ogle at his muscular arms, which were strong, sinewy and taut.

'Looks like your mum has a bumper crop of cards. Are you planning to have a birthday party?'

He raised his arm and waved it around with a dramatic flourish.

'Should additional entertainment be needed, I have a wide variety of anecdotes on my exploits and adventures which could be yours for the price of a good dinner. And, seeing as it is your mum, I would be willing to throw in a free slide-show on your computer of the knitting and textile crafts of South America, India, Nepal and several parts of East Africa.'

'All for the sake of a good meal? Well, that is a good offer.' Mimi smiled, but she did not dare look at him. 'Sorry, no party.'

'Don't say that I have missed it. I was looking

forward to meeting your mother and finding out where you got your good looks from. Maybe *she'll* see that I have potential in the fashion trade.'

Mimi's hands found things to do with two large boxes of knitting-kit bags which had just been delivered in the post.

Time to say it out loud and move on.

'Sorry to disappoint you, but my mother passed away six months ago. A stroke; she had been ill for a while. All her friends agreed that we should remember her birthday. That's all.'

She inhaled a long breath and turned back to face Hal, but as she did so her hand caught one of the cartons which overturned onto the floor with a soft thud, breaking the tense atmosphere.

Hal was there to pick it up before she had fully realised that he had moved, so that when she swung back down he was there by her side.

'Thank you; how clumsy of me,' Mimi whispered.

'You are most welcome,' he replied in a low voice that she had never heard him use before. 'I am very sorry for your loss—and for putting my big foot in it. You must miss her a great deal.'

Mimi tried to smile bravely, but gave up. She hated false sentiment.

'Yes, I do,' she replied, standing straight and picking up one of the bags.

'I only wish that she had lived long enough to see my first collection. We worked on the designs together, you know. Just talking them through and drawing sketches late into the evening, or out on the patio in the summer,' she babbled, only too aware that she was in great danger of allowing her grief to come out in front of Hal—and she would not do that. Her grief was so very private, and she had learned to guard her feelings and keep them tightly bound to her, away from the world, afraid to show any sign of weakness or lack of resolve.

'Mimi.'

'Certainly enough to keep me busy. Especially in the long winter evenings.'

'Mimi.' His right hand was on her forearm now, holding her. Supporting her. Giving her strength.

'It's okay. You're okay,' he said in a warm, calm voice which was like a soothing balm. 'I love the fact that you want to celebrate her birthday and keep that connection real. Perhaps I should have done that for Poppy when our parents died.'

He looked up. 'They were killed during an earthquake in Turkey. She was only ten when it happened, and I was not exactly the sentimental type. It might have helped her. So good on you for making the effort. I'm sure your mother must have been a remarkable woman.'

Mimi swallowed down her quivering emotion and braved a half-smile, embarrassed at making such a display of herself in front of a relative stranger.

'She was. And now it is my turn to be sorry. Your parents would have been proud of what you and Poppy have achieved.'

'Me? Not so sure about that. I'm just a vagrant compared to the powerhouse you have built up here. Let me see—business owner, designer, teacher and apparently you can knit things. Four jobs; that takes some doing.'

Mimi smiled back, pleased that he was shifting the subject, and grateful to him for recognising that she would rather not talk about such painful things. 'Thank you for that, but I would hardly call you a vagrant. In fact, I suspect you could clean up quite nicely.'

His hand was still resting lightly on her arm,

but as she looked up into his face and pressed the palms of both hands onto the front of his T-shirt she sensed his fingers sliding slowly down onto her waist in silence.

Instantly she froze, fearful at the totally unexpected but oh-so-welcome physical contact, then pulled slowly away inch by inch, breaking the connection.

She did not *do* intimate. Never. She'd no plans to start now, even if her body sometimes yearned for the physical comfort of another human being.

Her mother had been a warm, extrovert Italian who'd adored holding and hugging her tight with delicious cuddles while her father had looked on— calm, quiet, reserved, just as loving, but without the need to be constantly reaching out for the touch of another person.

It was at times like this that she regretted being more like her dad, but she had learned over these last hard years that her poor heart needed to be kept safe and guarded behind locked doors if she had any chance of surviving. And not even Hal Langdon had the key to open it, even if he was knocking rather loudly.

The air between them seemed concentrated and

heavy, and it was Mimi who dared to speak first, desperate to shift the conversation away from her.

'Why are you being so hard on yourself, Hal? You must have done and seen some remarkable things in your work. I envy you that freedom to go and do what you please on your own. Although, I should imagine that it must be a lonely life some-times.'

Mimi was so close that she could not block out the look in his startled eyes. His mouth looked so soft and wide; lush. He already had the slightest hint of stubble, so what must the rest of his body be like?

No; she couldn't think about what was below the chest hairs already curling out from the V of his white shirt.

In a fraction of a second, when their eyes met, Mimi felt something connect in her gut, as though a tough wire had been hooked into each of them, drawing them closer and closer together. And all of the time her eyes were fixed onto his face, watch-ing as Hal took a deep breath and as words formed in that amazing mouth.

'Yes, it can be very lonely at times.'

The cable tightened and Mimi moved a little

closer, anxious not to break the mental connection,
but still holding back with all of her might from
actually touching him.

'At times?' she whispered with a questioning lilt.

'I have been to some of the most beautiful places
on earth. It makes it extra special when you have
someone with you to share those moments. Do you
know what I mean?'

'Yes. I know exactly what you mean,' Mimi replied in a voice so soft that it could have been a
whisper. Hal leant back against her desk, slipped
his left hand out from his crutch and stretched his
fingers up into her hair, drawing her even closer towards him so that his warm soft lips gently glided
over her forehead.

Before she could change her mind, Mimi Fiorini
Ryan closed her eyes and luxuriated in the precious, fleeting contact with Hal. Her skin warmed
to the heat of his mouth on her temples, and her
nostrils filled with a heady smell of coffee and
musky aftershave.

She let the pressure of his breath on her face, and
the scent and sensation of his body, warm every
cell before she finally pulled her head away.

Hal looked down at her with those caramel eyes,

his chest responding to his faster breathing, and whispered, 'Sharing,' before moving his hand higher onto her waist. His arm formed a tight circle, locking her close to his body as his fingers moved up in gentle circles, caressing the small of her back.

The combined sensations were so overpowering that when the telephone rang on her office desk Mimi thought that it might just be the sound of the blood pounding with the ringing in her ears. It was only when the answer machine kicked in that some part of her brain which was not totally intoxicated by the power of the man who was holding her so gently in his strong arms wondered if perhaps she should answer it.

She decided that, no, whatever and whoever it was in the outside world could wait.

'Hi, Miss Ryan. Paul here. Just following up on the student graduate show. Sorry to bother you, but my editor has asked me to extend my report into a feature article. Is there any chance that I could have an exclusive interview in the next hour or so back at the gallery? I'll be here until two. Looking forward to hearing from you soon. Bye for now.'

Hal's hands froze for just a second as he looked

over her shoulder towards the answer machine, then dropped away from her body faster than she thought possible, leaving her reeling, bereft and desperate to reconnect.

But Hal was already reaching for his crutch. 'The hotel,' he said with a short cough. 'Really need to see the hotel. Check out the stage and things. Um, right; best to go now. Back soon. See you later.' And before Mimi could catch her breath to reply he had slung his camera bag over one shoulder, forced his left arm into his crutch and was out of the room.

She waved a faint farewell to his retreating back just as it slipped through into the knitting shop. 'See you later. And, wow.'

Four hours later Hal's leg was aching so much that no amount of massage was going to help. He hobbled through the knitting shop, nodding to the customers as he did so, until he was able to close the door behind him and enter the quiet and controlled world of Mimi's studio.

After so many hours on his feet at the conference hotel Poppy had booked for the fashion show, he needed a hot shower, a good meal and sleep—lots of sleep.

And most of all he needed to calm down and relax somewhere quiet.

Poppy had been right when she'd said there was still a lot to do before the show. The hotel was quite capable of organising a runway; that was no problem. What Poppy could not have predicted was that the hotel would start their major renovation-work a few weeks earlier than planned and somehow forget to inform Poppy of that fact.

The result was that most of Hal's visit to the events manager had been interrupted by electrical and air-conditioning faults, and they had lost power to that part of the building twice.

The only good news was that, as part-recompense and after much negotiation, the organiser had agreed to allow Hal to use the elegant reception rooms for most of Sunday afternoon for his photo shoot for Mimi's final two evening dresses.

It had been an exhausting couple of hours and his body was already telling him that perhaps he should be taking it easier after months of convalescence. He had almost fallen into the taxi cab bringing him back here to the calm and tranquil space he needed.

And to Mimi Ryan.

He hadn't planned to hold Mimi so tenderly earlier, or to touch her, or to feel her skin and inhale the sweet perfume she wore which infused her clothes and hair.

But when he'd touched her face, sensed the intensity of her grief for her mother...?

Of course he could have resisted. Only she had felt so right at the time.

What was it about Mimi that made his heart sing when they had only just met?

Fool!

Well, that had to stop. He had to pull back and stay objective. He had nothing to offer this woman, and he knew to his cost just how destructive and overwhelming the power of love could be. He had seen it with Tom and he did not want any part of it.

He only hoped that this girl with the tender heart of gold would understand that the problem lay with him and not her.

There was a shuffling noise from the patio, and as Hal looked up at the winding staircase that led up to Mimi's apartment he was struck by the most severe test to his resolve yet.

Hal stumbled out onto the patio in the growing shadows of the late-afternoon sunlight and stared in astonishment at the lovely meal laid out on the patio table, with a dash of awe added to the mix.

Mimi had changed out of her coral knitted top into a very long and very loud blue-and-green-patterned light blouse with sparkly bits in it. Her hair was loose and unkempt, and the only colour in her face was a slight moustache of what looked like chocolate on her upper lip.

This was probably why he just stood there in silence, grinning at her instead of saying something sensible and intelligent.

'What?' Mimi asked, looking behind her. 'What's so funny?'

Hal gestured to his own upper lip with one finger, and instantly Mimi did the same with a loud groan.

'Oh, no! The icing didn't set on Mum's birthday cake. Please, come and sit down while I make myself respectable.'

'Don't rush on my account,' he replied with a smirk as she jogged away from him.

Hal settled onto the patio chair, stretched his leg out and admired the patio in the fading sunlight. The small round table had been set with a white embroidered cloth. Terracotta plant-pots were brimming over with brightly coloured flower arrangements and trailing ivy, against the golden sandstone of the patio flagstones. Everywhere he looked there was colour and texture.

It was a quiet and lovely spot. Calm. Tranquil. He could almost feel the tension ebbing away from him as his shoulders dropped lower and his breathing calmed.

Mimi walked back towards him, wiping her mouth on a tissue.

'One of these days,' Mimi said, 'I might invest in air-conditioning but until then I shall have to learn to live with molten-chocolate icing.'

Hal held his gaze as Mimi bustled between the small studio kitchen and the table. She had been pretty in the studio but here, with the faint sunlight coming onto one side of her smooth face, on the gold chestnut of her hair, with the palest of green reflections in her eyes, she was absolutely stunning. His camera was on his bed but to move now would mean destroying the moment.

Suddenly Hal was very glad that he had come to London and this knitting shop—to be able to be here, at this precious second of time, no matter what happened to their relationship going forward.

Okay, he would have to work like crazy to make good his promise to his sister, but right now at this moment he was off-duty.

Mimi laughed and looked into Hal's face with a sly grin. 'Can I make a suggestion? Why don't we take ten minutes and enjoy our dinner? Then we can talk about the show and what we do next. I think we both deserve a break after the day we have had. Do we have a deal?'

Hal looked into those eyes and decided that anything that would keep him sitting at this table for a moment longer than before would be an excellent deal.

'I am powerless to resist any beautiful lady—especially if she is offering me food. I would be honoured.' Then he relaxed and rubbed his hands together. 'Yes, of course. And I'm starving. What have you got?'

'Rocket, sliced tomatoes, fresh mozzarella; Parmesan, if you need it. Bread's just here; you can cut your own just how you like it. And, of course, coconut cake with chocolate icing. Help yourself to all and any. Oh, almost forgot.'

Mimi jumped up, strolled over to a bushy green plant in a bright blue planter and snipped off a couple of stems. The smell hit Hal before she sat down.

'You have fresh basil!' Hal said, watching her tear the leaves across the platter of salad. 'It smells wonderful.'

Mimi tore a few of the large leaves into shreds and scattered them on his plate, before using a large china spoon to serve him a generous portion of cheese and salad.

'Try it with these buffalo tomatoes. My local greengrocer buys them from a farmer just north of Palermo. In the summer, the plum varieties come from the mainland. None of *these* boys have seen a greenhouse or chemicals. Don't worry; I did wash the Sicilian insect life off them first and gave them a chance to warm up a bit.'

Mimi sat back down and dipped her slice of sourdough briefly in the basil dressing before looking up at Hal, who had gone silent.

'Oh,' she whispered. She chewed the cheese, tomato and basil combination. Her eyes were half-closed, and a look of relaxed contentment flooded into her face.

So that's what you look like when you're happy. You should do this more often, Mimi Ryan—preferably when you are looking at me!

Mimi opened her eyes to find Hal smiling across at her, and immediately brought her hand to her mouth to wipe away the dregs of salad dressings, but he was too fast for her. Without planning it, or hesitation, Hal reached out and wiped the pad of his thumb along the side of her cheek. Her mouth was half-open and so inviting that he struggled to slide his thumb away.

'No. You're fine just as you are. No need to change a thing,' Hal said, still looking at Mimi. Her neck was flushed an interesting shade of red and her upper lip was twitching as though something had triggered a reaction she had not been expecting. But when she looked up into his eyes through long, dark eyelashes the smile and pleasure in the corners of her eyes was real.

'Thank you.' She used the tip of her tongue to wipe away traces from her lip and Hal's breathing quickened. 'And you've gone quiet again. I'm already embarrassed about what happened earlier. Tell me what you're thinking—please?' Mimi pleaded, her head tilted to one side.

Loading his lunch plate with food seemed to be the perfect excuse for not looking at Mimi directly as Hal took his time to answer.

'I was thinking that you enjoy good food. And I am also thinking that you have nothing whatsoever to be embarrassed about. I am single, over twenty-one and frequently accused of allowing my instincts—and my will to run things the way I want them—to get the better of me. If anything, I should be the one who should be embarrassed at my lack of self-control. There; does that make you feel better? And you were the one who asked me what I was thinking.'

She had stopped chewing but was still watching him cut more bread.

'Yes, I did, didn't I? Perhaps that was a bit...'

'Reckless? It seems that I am having a terrible influence on you, Miss Ryan.'

He lifted up the bread and cheese to his mouth and was just about to bite into it when he stopped, looked into her eyes, tilted his head in an exact copy of how she looked and whispered, 'Now you have to tell me what *you* are thinking.'

'I fell right into that one, didn't I, bossy boots?' Mimi replied. She put her knife and fork back on her plate, focused on moving them an inch apart then back together, then apart again, before she spoke.

'Okay. I was thinking that I might be single, over twenty-one and capable of making my own decisions, but I am *not* used to allowing my instincts to get the better of me.' She shrugged her shoulders at him. 'Perhaps that's why I am embarrassed about pouncing on you. Sorry about that.'

Hal chewed longer than necessary so that he could calm himself and keep a straight face. 'It was my pleasure. Please feel free to pounce at will. But that does mean you have given me a huge challenge.'

He smiled across at her and winked. 'How am I going to be able to prevent myself from pouncing right back over the next few days when we are going to be working together? Any ideas?'

Mimi tried with all her might not to look shell-shocked at the outrageous question Hal had just asked her—and failed.

He needed self-control to stop himself from holding her again? *Her?*

This was some kind of crazy joke—it had to be.

'That is very flattering, Hal, but I don't think we are going to have much spare time over the next week, do you? There is so much to do I can hardly think. We have a lot to sort out.'

'I agree. But you need to help me understand something,' he replied in a lighter voice. 'Tom Harris was my friend, and I want to do whatever I can to support the foundation he started. But why is this event so important to you? There have to be other opportunities for up-and-coming designers in a city the size of London. Please; I would like to know. Why do you want to do this so badly?'

Why was this event so important to her?

The full story; the truth; she was nowhere near ready to tell Hal the truth.

But he was the gatekeeper on the door to her dreams, and if she had to share some of her life with him it would be worth it.

'You're right. It might help if you understood why I am putting myself through all of this when there is already enough going on in my life.'

Hal nodded and stretched his legs out under the table. 'Not might help—it *will* help. I have time; start when you ready. I need to know everything.'

Mimi inhaled a long, deep breath, took one look into those intense brown eyes which were focused unblinkingly on her face, and tried to drop away some of the tension that was building in her shoulders.

Where to start?

She got up from the table and returned a few seconds later holding a glossy fashion magazine in one hand and a framed picture in the other.

'Have you ever heard of the Italian couture house of Fiorini?'

Hal's lips twisted in surprise. 'Fiorini? Yes, I think Poppy worked for them in Milan when she was a teenager. She loved the evening-wear.'

'That was their speciality. If you needed a red-carpet gown or cocktail dress, then Fiorini was the only place to go. They used to produce some lovely work.'

'Okay, that's all very interesting, but what has that got to do with Mimi Ryan?'

Her response was to turn the fashion magazine around so that Hal could see the cover photo of a handsome, sophisticated man. The headline read: *Fiorini International. A luxury brand taking over the world.*

He glanced at the photo once and waited.

'Meet my cousin,' Mimi said in a low voice. 'Luca Fiorini. The current CEO of Fiorini International.'

Mimi could not resist smiling at her mother's picture before lowering it flat onto the table.

'My mother's full name was Talia Isabella Mimi Costa Fiorini Ryan. And she was the great-granddaughter of the founder of the Fiorini dynasty.' Mimi smiled across at Hal. 'So, you see? *I am* a Fiorini. Body and soul.'

CHAPTER SIX

'MAY I?' Hal asked, gesturing towards the silver-framed photograph, and Mimi handed him the picture.

The very pretty young woman he was looking at was medium height with slim arms and legs; her silk summer dress highlighted delicate features which screamed elegance and class.

Mimi's mother was standing in a stunning garden with a lake view on one side and snow-capped mountains on the other. Yet her expression was focused completely towards the camera.

'How old was your mother when this photograph was taken?' he asked.

'Oh, about thirty. My father took the picture. I think they had been invited to some sort of family party in Milan and they weren't enjoying themselves very much.'

Hal passed the photograph back. 'She looks like a very determined lady. And very beautiful.'

Mimi was silent for a moment as she replaced the picture at the end of the table.

Oh, no, Hal thought. *Got it wrong again.* 'Now I really do have to apologise for saying the wrong thing,' he said in a low voice.

Mimi looked directly at him. 'Actually, just the opposite. She *was* very determined. And, yes, she could be quite formidable, especially where my dad and I were concerned. It's just that—' Mimi glanced back at the picture '—I think that you are the first person who has looked into that face and recognised that in her. She would have liked that. She always preferred straight talking. I suppose I get that from her.'

'Well, you are a Fiorini. What did Poppy say when you told her about your family connection? It would be terrific on the adverts.'

'Poppy doesn't know,' Mimi replied in a low voice. Then she squeezed her lips together and gave a small shrug. 'It was my decision not to tell her. In fact, you are the first person I've told about my links to the Fiorini family. And I've only done that because I believe that I can trust you to keep what I am telling you a secret. I really do not want to use the Fiorini connection to publicise the fundraiser. Do you think that you can do that?'

'If that is what you want, but I am still confused. It sounds like you have a wonderful heritage behind you which you could use to your advantage. Your collection could attract a lot more attention if they knew that Studio Designs had a Fiorini name attached to it. Why the secrecy?'

Mimi straightened her back and lifted her chin. 'I have been working all of my life to get as far away from the Fiorini family as possible and stand on my own two feet, Hal. I started at the bottom and made my own way in the world. This first collection of clothes has taken me ten years of hard work in difficult circumstances to put together. These are not just clothes—they are my future goals and dreams all combined into a few pieces of cloth. That probably doesn't make sense, but that is how I feel about the work.'

Hal sat back in his own chair and nodded. 'Actually, it makes perfect sense.' Then he leant both elbows on the table so that he could grin at Mimi as she ate her cake. 'Don't apologise for being passionate about what you do and what you want in your life. It's only natural that you

are going to get a little carried away trying to explain it.'

'And what makes you get carried away, Hal?'
Mimi said, her voice low and intimate; she was
very conscious that their hands were only inches
apart from each other.

'Way too many things. But let's start with chocolate icing,' he replied and leaning forward, he
raised one finger and slowly wiped it along the
edge of the cake plate, before popping his chocolate coated fingertip into his mouth.

It only took a fraction of a second, and it was
the most sensual thing Mimi had ever seen in her
life.

For a moment their eyes locked together.

But chocolate was not what Hal was thinking
about. Not at all.

The need took his breath away and left him
floundering, helpless.

What if she wanted him as much as he wanted
her at this minute? That could only spell trouble—
for both of them.

Hal broke the mood by looking away first.

Then he made the fatal mistake of glancing back and fell dizzyingly into Mimi's green,

amber-flecked eyes. Eyes which called to him with a message that his heart could not ignore: *I like you. A lot.*

Oh, no. Not Mimi. Not now.

Doomed.

Without a second's hesitation, he leant forward just an inch and started to angle his head so that their noses would not clash; their eyes were still locked. His tongue moistened over his upper lip, and hers instinctively did the same. His gaze glanced from her mouth back to her eyes as his hand came up to cradle the back of her head, smoothing down the hair, caressing the warm skin between her neck and ear. Suddenly he wanted, needed, to crush his mouth against hers and taste her sweetness, life and passion.

He could sense that her breathing speeded up in anticipation of his kiss, her eyes half-closed at the pleasure to come. She wanted him to kiss her.

Only he forced himself to pull back in silence, his hand dropping back to the table. But his eyes never left Mimi's face as she sat back, her face flushed, her chest rising and falling with the intensity of the moment. All of the passion and energy that he had only glimpsed before was there for him to see in her lovely face, making it even more difficult for him to fight against what his heart was telling him.

After so many months of guarding his very words and feelings, this overwhelming desire and need to hold and comfort Mimi was going to have to be yet another challenge to overcome if he had any hope of getting through this next week.

Hal sucked in a breath of the cool, cleansing evening air and said in as calm a voice as he could manage, 'There is one question which only you can answer. And it will impact everything else we do in the next week.'

Mimi took a breath and sat in silence while Hal leant forward and said in a low voice, 'Don't you think it's time you showed me the actual clothes?'

In reply Mimi's eyes grew even wider. She opened her mouth, then closed it again, pressing her lips together.

Hal chewed on the inside of his cheek, suddenly anxious. Perhaps his desperate plan to change the subject was backfiring.

'The clothes?' she murmured. 'You mean the collection for the show?'

Hal nodded, desperate to refocus on something

concrete and specific, anything that would distract him from the fact that he was still within touching distance of the first woman he had wanted to kiss, hold and come to know in a very long time. Which was probably why he rushed his words and spoke far more loudly than he had intended.

'The catalogue for the show has to be with the printers by Tuesday morning at the latest. I was hoping to stage the photo shoot for those last two outfits some time tomorrow—if that is okay with you?'

'Tomorrow?' Mimi's head came up and her eyebrows lifted. 'That would be great, but what about the venue and the models?'

Hal nodded and gestured with his hand palm-down. 'I've just come back from the hotel and I'll be seeing Lola and Fifi later tonight.' Then his voice softened. 'It would be a great help if I knew what I was going to photograph.'

Mimi blinked several times and seemed to shuffle on her chair. She shot him a shy glance through her eyelashes and there was something in that one glance that shook him slightly. Hal had seen that look before in the faces of adventurers—and it was usually right before they jumped off a mountain they knew little about with a parachute on their back which they had not packed and checked themselves.

She was nervous. Anxious. Possibly terrified. And that confused him even more.

'You did say that the dresses were ready, didn't you? Because I can move the photo shoot to Monday if you need more time.'

'Oh, no, no,' Mimi rushed with a shake of her head. 'That's not it. The dresses are finished and I'm thrilled with them. It's just that…' She sighed and swallowed several times, unable to continue.

'Go on,' Hal said, leaning forward in support. 'It's just that…?'

'The students helped me with some of the day suits but I've worked all of the evening-wear on my own. Poppy saw the first pieces but I left these two dresses to the end. They were special and I wanted them to be so perfect. In fact, I want them to be on the front cover of the catalogue. That's why I have spent every spare minute of the past three weeks reworking the designs until I can't see any way I can improve them. These two gowns are probably the finest work I've ever done.'

Hal smiled across at her. 'Then I can't wait to see them.'

'That's just it,' she whispered. 'You will be the first person to see the finished gowns, and I am nervous. Really nervous.'

She lifted her head and looked out across the patio to the tops of the trees beyond her gate. 'Before you say anything, I know that sounds totally ridiculous. I know that my Fiorini family won't be there, but I just can't seem to take them out of the picture. They made the finest evening-wear in the world, and here am I, trying to create something new under my own name when I have the weight of all of that heritage hanging over me.'

'Is that why you don't want to have the Fiorini name on the posters? In case the critics compare your work to the Fiorini couture clothes? Because it will come out eventually, you know.'

Her brow tightened and she sought out his eyes, willing him to understand why this was so important to her without her having to say the words. 'You are probably right,' she replied in a low, hoarse voice. 'I just want this chance to stand up on my own and show what I am capable of. That's all. Just one chance.'

Mimi's gentle vulnerability hit Hal hard in the pit of his stomach, setting his skin tingling and heart racing. He had once believed that he knew about taking risks in his life, but this girl's heart and soul were exposed for anyone to see if they cared to look. She probably had no idea how endearing and how special her simple wish to be recognised felt to him at that moment. It would be so easy to hurt her with meaningless words of reassurance or false hope.

Suddenly he felt as though he was standing shoulder deep in dangerous waters and it had just started to rain.

Feelings so fresh, sharp and new assailed his heart and begged to be expressed by taking Mimi in his arms and holding her until she understood that she could never be anything less than she was capable of. He had been guarding his heart even before Tom's death, and now when he needed it to be strong and resilient it was letting him down, broken and shattered by one look into the eyes of a girl called Mimi Ryan.

Seconds stretched to minutes as Mimi sought out an answer in his face. Time enough for his brain to kick in and regain possession of his body.

'If you would prefer to talk me through the collection, or show me your sketches, I would be okay with that. I am happy to wait until the girls are wearing your dresses tomorrow, if that would make you more comfortable.'

She slowly raised her head, and as she looked into his face and made eye contact he saw something so intense in her eyes that it took his breath away.

Self-doubt, fear, deep loneliness and need were all there in that one single glance.

'These clothes have taken ten years of my life,' she whispered, her voice low and gentle and as warm as a summer breeze on his brow. 'And now I have to show them to the world, for better or for worse.'

She lifted her head and braved a weak smile. 'I know that I am being totally pathetic.'

He felt her breath come in short gasps as she searched his face, as though looking for some kind of answer or hidden truth or reassurance. 'And what if it is for worse, Hal? What if it turns out that I am a self-delusional old bat and the designs stink? Then what? Where do I go from there?'

Hal tipped up Mimi's chin with the back of one finger so that he could smile into her startled eyes.

'We all fear risking the thing we love best in the world, Mimi. It's what makes us human. We take a risk every single time we step forward and show some of our true selves to the world, knowing that we could be rejected or humiliated.'

Two of his fingers flicked stray strands of her tousled hair back over one ear as he spoke into the air above her head. 'You are not alone. And you won't be on the day. I'll be there with Poppy. And here's a promise: nobody will dare to criticise your clothes when I am on the scene. Right? Of course right!'

Hal stood back a step and gave a small, casual shrug but his voice was steady, calm, clear and very, very challenging. 'We are going to prove to the world that the woman who wears your clothes can do and go and be whoever she wants to be. *That* is what we are going to do in the show. *That* is the theme. Fabulous and elegant clothes meant for real women in the real world.'

Then his mouth lifted into a grin and he winked. 'And I know exactly how we are going to go about it.'

Mimi blinked several times to clear the sleep out of her eyes with a wide yawn as she sipped her

breakfast coffee and looked out over her neighbours' gardens which were illuminated by the low,
early-morning light.

Reshaping the fall of a pair of elegant wide-leg
trousers had taken her until well after midnight,
but even when she had eventually collapsed into
bed she had spent most of the night listening out
for any sounds to indicate that Hal had moved into
his new studio bedroom.

Which might account for the extra-large bags
under her eyes, and her inability to stop yawning
for more than a few minutes at a time. She really
did need to catch up with her sleep some time
before the weekend, or she would be even more
of an emotional wreck than she was now.

Hal had taken her spare back-gate and patio-door
keys so he was free to come and go as he wanted.
But the very idea of having Hal sneaking in and
out of the studio without her knowing about it was
still more than a little disturbing.

She was simply not used to having someone else
sharing her home.

Her family had never had guests stay over. Ever.
The fact that there were only two bedrooms was

one reason, but her parents had loved their privacy. It was one more thing she had inherited from them.

The only person she had ever shared a room with was her mother, and that was only after she had started sleepwalking. No girly sleepovers. And she had not been given any choice about living at home when she was at college because of the lack of funds and the fact that she could easily commute in each day by bus.

Hal Langdon was her first houseguest. And she had no idea what to expect.

Did he expect her to cook all of his meals, or entertain his friends and colleagues?

She sighed and raised her arms above her head to try and release some of the tension in her shoulders. They would probably have to establish some sort of ground rules as soon as possible.

That must be the reason she was so nervous—the domestic arrangements. That was all. It had nothing at all to do with the fact that macho, handsome, totally dreamworthy, fascinating, and amazingly kissable Hal Langdon would be staying in her house for the rest of the week, working in her studio. And standing next to her during her day, looking at her, talking to her. Pressing his body next to hers.

Generally throwing her normal calm and orderly life into total chaos.

Mimi sank down onto her breakfast-table chair, stretched out her arms and dropped her head onto them.

This was all her fault.

She was the one who had suggested Langdon Events rent out her studio space. There was no point in kidding herself she had done it for the rent, although she could certainly use the money. No. This was about fear. Ten years of fraught and exhausting work had gone into realising her dream, and the very idea that she would be excluded from the organisation gave her the shivers.

Poppy Langdon had offered her a golden chalice and she had been only too willing to drink from it, not knowing the full consequences.

The truth was more challenging than she would admit—to anyone. Deep-seated fears combined with long-term lack of sleep and poor confidence had driven her to take decisions which would have terrified her only a year earlier.

Fear had driven her to hand control over her future to another person.

Lifting her head a few inches, the first thing she saw through her half-open eyes was her mother's photograph.

Look at the muddle I have got myself into now, Mum.

The only reply was from the steady ticking of the old wind-up clock against the silence of the morning. Rhythmical and consistent, in tune with the beat of her heart. Bird song filtered in from the other side of the glass and faint rays of morning sunshine crept over the trees and brought hope and energy to the space. And to her spirit.

She could do this. She could dress and eat breakfast as though this was just a normal Sunday morning. Then she would start work on the project she had thrashed out, one step at a time, just as Hal had suggested. Same as normal.

Except for the fact that things were very far from normal.

Starting with the fact that Hal Langdon might be sleeping a few feet below her at that very minute.

Sniffing away her anxiety, Mimi blinked again

and ruffled through the papers to find her list of things to do for the day.

It wasn't there, because she had left it on her desk in the studio late last evening after she had printed out the draft version of the catalogue Poppy had sent her for the show.

Drat! The printers needed the catalogue by Tuesday at the latest and there was still work to do, even without the shots of her evening dresses. She would have to go and find it.

Mimi stretched up her head and found that by drawing the curtain slightly to one side she could actually see most of the patio from where she was sitting. There was no sign of movement or Hal.

In which case there would be no harm in her peeping inside the studio. It was hardly likely that Hal would be awake and moving out of Poppy's apartment before 7:00 a.m. on a Sunday morning. He would never know that she had been there. But she had better do it fast before he woke up. In fact, she had better do it now, even if she was still in her pyjamas.

* * *

The patio stones were cool under her bare feet as Mimi skipped down the stairs from her apartment and stepped out to cross over to the studio.

Mimi quickly looked from side to side to make sure that nobody was watching, and then scolded herself for being so foolish. This was her house!

Nevertheless she did mince slowly up towards the patio doors and gave a gentle cough before slowly opening the doors and peeking inside. No movement.

Feeling braver, she stepped inside the workshop then stopped still. The découpage screen had been pulled away and she could see inside Hal's short-term bedroom—if she wanted.

She wanted.

Curiosity won. The area was not as messy as she had feared. On top of the single mattress was a well-used sleeping bag. A large rucksack was stuffed into the far corner next to the bed, under a small portable picnic table just large enough for a travel alarm-clock, laptop computer, a notebook and pens. Hal's camera bag was on the floor on the other side of the bed, with his shoes, jeans, biker jacket and his watch and mobile phone. And a very familiar metal crutch.

Oh, no. He was here!

At the same instant Mimi heard a low chuckle behind her back and whipped around.

There, leaning against the door to the tiny bathroom, was Hal Langdon, wearing an amused expression on his face.

That was just about all he was wearing.

A pair of black boxer shorts hung from his hips in a casual, lopsided style.

He had crossed one sturdy muscular leg across the other, highlighting his sinewy calves, slim ankles and long brown toes. She decided to ignore the black big-toe nail and the scratches and scrapes which ran up the side of one leg as though he had fallen from a motorcycle or been dragged down a rock face.

That must have hurt!

His other leg looked thinner with white threadmarks crawling up from the inflatable boot which encased his lower left-leg.

She ignored these because the focus of her attention was higher up as Hal began to pull a black cotton T-shirt over his head, and she stared quite brazenly at his remarkable broad, powerful chest.

It was only a few seconds. But they were quite memorable seconds.

She knew that Poppy was in her late twenties so Hal could not be more than early thirties but every one of those years was evident in that body. Scars and more scrape-marks picked out one side of his ribs. His firm, tight abdominals ended in a sharp V on his hips.

If Hal Langdon ever fancied a change of direction to become a swimwear model, he would have no shortage of offers—even with the scars.

She was looking at an athlete who was totally relaxed in his own skin, unafraid, and unaware of how very, very masculine and attractive he truly was.

It made her feel totally inadequate.

Men like Hal Langdon were not frightened of water or the huge spiders that lived in her bath.

She was almost disappointed when Hal tugged his T-shirt down over his chest. Just knowing that his body looked like that under his clothing was going to have to be enough to keep her going for the rest of the day.

'Morning,' he yawned with one hand over his mouth. 'Hope I didn't wake you.'

'Not at all,' she managed to say, pretending to be casual and matter-of-fact, as though she spoke to Adonis-handsome men with 'run your fingers through me, please' bed hair every morning of the week. 'In fact, I didn't hear you at all during the night. Were you very late?'

The answer was a quick snort. 'Make that very early. You will be pleased to know that I managed to talk Poppy's flatmates into modelling those last two evening dresses today, but I had to wait until three this morning to do it. I gave up trying to sleep at that point and headed over here instead.'

Mimi's eyes widened. 'That's great, but do you mean you have only just got here? Aren't you exhausted?'

Hal grinned. 'A lack of sleep and clubbing friends are not the best combination, but there are compensations.'

Mimi looked at him quizzically. 'Compensations?'

'Well, it is not every day that I have the opportunity to see the lovely Mimi Ryan in her pyjamas, and it looks like straight from her bed—which is a good thing! And, by the way, any time you would like a personal tour of my bedroom behind that screen all you have to do is ask.' And he gave

Mimi a small wink and twitch of his lips, then seemed to delight in hearing her squeal and scamper away to get dressed.

CHAPTER SEVEN

'I STILL can't believe that you persuaded Lola to braid pink ribbons in her hair. She looked fantastic against that Chinese hand-painted wallpaper.'

'Not pink,' Mimi teased as Hal pointed to the computer monitor. 'They call it *nude* these days. I made the ribbons using the same fabric as the dress, and once I explained the Edwardian-aristocrat effect I was looking for she was a total professional. She even let Fifi make a little bow at the side. Here; you can just see it at the nape of Lola's neck when her hair was up.'

Mimi huddled next to Hal and stared in delight at the screen as he skipped from digital photograph to photograph of Lola and Fifi taken at the photo shoot earlier that evening.

'You know, I have never seen these rooms in the hotel before,' Mimi added. 'Poppy and I only went to the main ballroom and that was weeks ago.

Look at those paintings and rich textiles! They are so elegant. It was a wonderful location—and just perfect for these two dresses. It was a great choice. Thanks, Hal.'

'Ah,' he snorted. 'Progress; you seem to like my work. I take this as a positive step.'

'Oh, you can use a camera, I'll give you that. The real problem is choosing which shot to use for the catalogue. It is so difficult. Wait—can I see that one?' Mimi rested her hand on Hal's arm for a fleeting moment and nodded to the screen.

Hal had captured a stunning full-length image of Lola from across the room as she gazed out of the casement window onto the busy London street. The sideways view displayed the cut of the dress, and the way the light caught the crystals and diamanté on the bodice was amazing. 'That is *wonderful*. That's it. That's the nude-pink evening-gown cover. Oh, that is so gorgeous.'

Hal lifted his right hand and blew on his finger-tips a couple of times before selecting the shot and pasting it onto the cover of the catalogue.

'I live to please. Glad that you like it.'

'Oh, you already know it's a brilliant shot,' Mimi hissed with a shake of her head. 'I heard you moving poor Lola an inch that way, and then the other way, so that the light was perfect. You've done this before, so you can stop being so modest. Poppy told me that you specialised in outdoor-action work; I hadn't expected you to love doing portraits, that's all.'

Hal shuffled on the chair as he transferred the image into the brochure and loaded another memory card into the computer. 'When I left university that was all I did for a while. I needed to earn enough money to fund my mountaineering trips, so my university pal Tom Harris begged and pleaded with his family until they finally relented and gave me a job in the family portrait studio.'

He turned his head to Mimi and grinned at her before going on. 'We used to come back from a climbing trip first thing Monday morning and go straight into the studio. I think some of the mothers were a little shocked to see a scratched and unshaven, grubby student taking photographs of their bouncing babies but the kids seemed to like us. We did well and I actually enjoyed it after a while.'

'Why? What did you like about it?' Mimi asked, fascinated by this glimpse into Hal's past.

'The people,' he answered without hesitation. 'Everyone has a camera these days, so when you go to a studio it is usually for some special occasion or important event. It was great fun.'

Mimi's eyebrows rose. 'You did weddings, didn't you?'

Hal threw back his head and laughed from deep in his belly.

'No. Tom and his dad did the wedding photography. It was great work. Although...' The smile dropped from Hal's face and he pressed his lips together before giving her a wry smile.

'When Tom asked me if I would take the photographs on his wedding day, I said no.'

Mimi gasped. 'Why?'

'I was going to be his best man. That was more than enough responsibility for me to handle on the day. Tom's dad was thrilled to take the job. It would have been a great day.'

Hal gestured towards the screen. 'But enough of that. Let's get back to Fifi. Powder-blue dress with those dangly things I always forget the name of. How about this one in front of the marble fireplace? It has to be a hit.'

'Bugle beads. Do you miss him—your friend Tom?'

She gazed into his face and waited patiently until he was ready to talk.

'Every day,' he replied, and then slowly turned to face her. 'Tom was not just a friend, he was more like the brother I never had. It doesn't get any easier, does it?'

'No. It doesn't get easier. I suppose you just get better at coping with the loss. And that is the best you can do. Take one day at a time and do the best you can.'

'Perhaps that's why we get on so well, you and I. We've both lost someone close to us in the last year. Maybe that is why we are clinging onto this charity show like a lifebelt, hoping that it will carry us out of the choppy waters. Maybe we should stick together and see where the current takes us. Together?'

The silence between them crackled with electricity. Mimi's heart rate soared as Hal's eyes stayed locked onto hers.

She was not going to speak. She could not. Dared not.

But, without hesitating or thinking through her

actions, Mimi reached out and wrapped her fingers around the back of Hal's hand just long enough for her to give it a gentle squeeze of comfort and support. Hal had asked her a question she could not find the words to answer. It seemed only right that she should reply with the most personal gift she could give him—her touch.

What she did not expect was that the intensity of that simple touch was so great he could have kissed her then and she would not have known the difference.

It was almost a relief to hear the telltale ringing of her mobile phone in her pocket. Very few people knew the number and she glanced quickly at the caller identity before sliding her hand away from Hal's and flicking the phone open. She felt the connection break the moment their skin ceased to be in contact, and it took a second for her to recognise that the person on the other end of the telephone was the conference organiser at the Grand Hotel where they were having the show.

'Oh, thank goodness.' A very relieved voice came down the phone. 'I am so sorry to disturb you so late in the evening, Miss Ryan, but I have been trying to get in touch with Poppy Langdon and she is not answering her phone.'

Mimi frowned at the tension in the normally terribly cool-and-collected voice and held the phone a little tighter, aware that Hal had not moved one inch and was still staring at her with that intense glare that made her squirm. 'Not a problem, but could I possibly call you back? I am right in the middle of a conversation and—'

'Oh, no, Miss Ryan. You don't understand; I have the most terrible news. There was a fire in the ballroom this evening. Our new smoke detectors were still being installed and the room was badly damaged before anyone knew what was going on. The ballroom is *ruined*. First from the fire then flooded with water from the fire hoses. It is going to take months to repair and we were lucky to save the rest of the hotel! Please accept my apologies but the ballroom is closed and we don't have another space to offer you. I am so sorry; we cannot hold your show at our hotel.'

'What? Say that again. No, wait.'

Mimi's left hand pressed hard against her heart, her fingers splayed out as if to hold down the fierce beat that was threatening to overwhelm her, just long enough to ask the question she was already dreading. Swallowing down her fear, she half-whispered, 'Are you telling me that the hotel is closed? That we can't use your ballroom for our fashion show?'

'All the furniture and fine decoration in the ball-room was completely burnt in the fire before the fire service arrived. I am so sorry, but there is nothing left. Nothing at all. Miss Ryan? Are you still there…?'

Everything became a blur and the room started spinning.

She had some vague impression that Hal was talking on her phone, but suddenly Mimi felt the need to collapse into a chair at the nearest work table and drop her head low between her knees. She breathed slowly in and out into a small brown-paper envelope she snatched from the table.

'Mimi? You okay?' Hal asked from somewhere vaguely above her head.

She shook her head once from side to side with-out looking up, then breathed deeper and faster into the envelope as the dizziness came back as she moved her head.

A hand touched her shoulder as Hal whispered, 'Cold water coming up. Be right back.'

Mimi took another breath and tried to calm her thumping heart, which was so loud inside her head she thought her brain would explode.

The bottom fell out of her stomach. She couldn't believe it.

Stupid! Stupid! Stupid girl for building up all of her hopes, dreams and ambition into one single fashion show! All she had wanted was those few precious hours when she could show what she was capable of. She had enjoyed today so much it had been like a happy dream. She should have known that a nightmare was only just around the corner.

She could cry.

A glass of water appeared on the floor in front of her as Hal bent down until he was at her level.

'Try this. Small sips.'

Mimi nodded in thanks and slowly swallowed down the cool liquid, pressing the dewy glass against her forehead for a few minutes until she was ready to sit up a little.

Hal was leaning against the other table, arms folded, simply watching her and still wearing his serious face.

'Better?'

Mimi licked her lips and took another sip before she was ready to reply. 'No.' She raised her head just high enough so that she could look at his face without throwing up. 'Well, that's it: no hotel. No show. It's over, Hal...' Her voice faded away to almost nothing, and she closed her eyes as she repeated, 'You might as well go home and forget the whole thing. Refund everyone who has bought tickets and tell them that the event is cancelled.'

'Who said anything about the show being cancelled?' Hal asked in a surprised voice. 'You may have noticed that there's more than one hotel in London. There are other venues and it's my job to track one down.'

Mimi tried to smile but her eyes refused to co-operate. 'Not with less than a week to go. All of the top locations are booked months if not years in advance. You will never be able to find a replacement venue at this short notice. And I am so very tired.

'No,' she whispered in a throat choked with bitter disappointment. 'Please do not give me false hopes. I would rather accept that the show is not going to happen this week and start thinking about a replacement. Perhaps in the winter; could we do that? Reschedule for later in the year? That gives us time to find the perfect location.'

To her astonishment, Hal shuffled over to her seat without his crutch and sat down next to her.

'We could do that, but for me that is second best. Langdon Events is responsible for finding a replacement location for the show. And that means me. Yes, I am disappointed too, but I will do my very best to find somewhere in this city for next Saturday.'

He took her hand in his and raised it to his lips so that he could kiss her knuckles and press her hand to his chest. 'The show will go on, Mimi. You can trust me on that.'

'I believe you will try your best, Hal. I really do. But I feel so powerless to help and I hate that. I am sorry, but I don't think I can cope with this news right now.'

'I know,' he replied with a smile, and flicked the hair back from her eyes. 'Why not have an early night? It's been an exhausting day for both of us. We can go through some of the options in the morning. Okay? Okay. Goodnight; try and get some sleep.'

* * *

Hal collapsed down into the patio chair and watched Mimi walk away from him across the patio and up the circular, winding staircase to her apartment. She was dragging her feet as though they were made of iron, and her head was down. After the wonderful day they had spent together, she looked defeated and deflated, a mere shadow of the woman he had come to care about.

Mimi was exhausted, physically and emotionally.

It was down to him to do something to put that right—and fast. But how?

Who did he know who could help? Poppy had to be his first port of call; she must have contacts in the city. He tried her mobile phone. There was no answer, so he left a message. This was no time for fake bravado about being the man who could do anything, and he would keep on ringing all night if that meant he could find an answer.

He had to do something to save the fundraiser for Tom, and the fashion show for Mimi. It meant so much to her; he could not let her down, not now. Not ever, if he had his way.

It was a shame his way was not working out very well. Not for this.

What had Tom used to say? 'There is always a

way. You just have to face your worst fears and get on and do it.'

The alternative was to accept defeat and fail. Fail Tom. Fail Poppy. And, most of all, fail Mimi, who was starting to believe in him and carry him along with her.

Hal blew out loud and scanned down the numbers on his phone until he found the name of the one person he had barely spoken to since Tom's funeral. Now she was the one person who might be able to save his skin and the fundraiser at the same time.

Aurelia DiMarco. Former supermodel and the woman Tom had loved more than his own life.

The woman Hal could not face, knowing that he held the real truth about Tom's death and could not tell her. Not until the time was right. And he was nowhere near ready to have that conversation with this beautiful woman who had sacrificed her career to live with Tom in a small mountain village. They had been such a happy couple; it broke his heart just to think about the pain she was going through.

Little wonder that she had moved back to New York to work for her family's chain of luxury hotels and restaurants. Aurelia knew hotel owners in most cities in the world, or at least who to call.

But he was going to have to speak to her first to ask for her help.

Hal's fingers paused over the call button for another second while he worked out what time it was in New York and whether he was ready for this call, but his finger pressed the button before he could change his mind.

She answered on the third ring.

'Aurelia? It's Hal. Yes, it has been a while. I know. Yes, thanks, the leg is a lot better. I'm calling about the fundraiser next weekend for Tom's foundation. Yes, I am looking forward to seeing you too, Aurelia, only we have a problem. And this time I need *your* help.'

Mimi turned over to find a comfy spot on her pillow; her eyes were closed tight against the morning light and she tugged the bed sheet higher around her shoulders. She was dreaming of classical music. Violins.

Unless… *Oh, no*, she groaned. Not a dream. It was the ring tone on her mobile phone.

Why was her phone ringing in the middle of the night?

Mimi half-creaked open one eye and peered at her clock over the top of the sheet. Oh. Was that 8:00 a.m.? Well, that was a first—she had actually slept through for at least twelve hours. She was normally awake and working well before seven. Except, of course, nothing seemed normal to her today. Nothing at all.

She squeezed her eyes together for a moment then blinked hard and pushed herself upright to answer her phone. It was a text message:

I have good news and breakfast. Coffee in ten minutes. H

Mimi closed her eyes, slid back under the bed clothes and groaned out loud. How dare Hal try and tempt her out of bed with vague promises of good news? Unless, of course, he had magically found a new venue for the fashion show, plus a whole forest of magic elves who were brilliant at stage management in a hurry. Now, that would be worth getting out of bed for.

Her phone rang again, but this time she scrabbled about for it on her bedside table and pulled it down to her level:

Make that very good news and chocolate crois-sants. And the coffee is already on.

'You have to love Monday mornings in this city.'

Hal hopped back into the tiny kitchen and emerged with a paper bag with the name of a famous French patisserie on the side. 'Chocolate croissants, fresh from a Covent Garden bakery. I was wondering if you might like one for breakfast with your coffee. Can I tempt you, Miss Ryan?'

'You can tempt me with *pain au chocolat* any day of the week,' Mimi replied, her hand covering her yawn. She was trying to resist the temptation to tug her dressing gown tighter up to the neck as she inhaled the mouth-watering aroma from the bag she accepted from him. 'Including Monday. Mmm. Lovely.'

She emptied the croissants onto a china plate. She rested her elbows on the patio table, tried to smile across at Hal and almost managed it. 'Sorry, I was so upset last night. It was hardly your fault that the hotel caught fire. On the other hand, if you have good news, now would be a really good time to share it.'

Hal pulled out the patio chair only inches away from hers and leant his elbows on the table so that their faces were practically touching as he smiled and said, 'I've found a replacement venue. And it is *amazing*. Do you think you could be ready to join me there at, say, eleven this morning?'

'A new venue?' She squealed and grabbed his arm without thinking, her whole body almost leaping up with excitement. 'Why on earth didn't you tell me earlier? Where? What kind of venue? A hotel? Conference centre? Which part of London? And how on earth did you manage to do that between nine yesterday evening and now?'

He held up one hand and shook his head slowly from side to side.

'Let's just say friends in high places. The place sounds terrific over the phone, but I need to head over and check it out before asking you to give it your final approval. Be ready to take a phone call with all of the details.'

Mimi felt her head strut forwards and her eyes open wide.

'Do you mean you won't even tell me where the new venue is?'

'What would be the fun in that?' Hal answered with a closed-mouth smile.

'So you just expect me to wait around here until you call? Why can't I come with you? That isn't fair.'

Hal nodded slowly. 'Don't worry; I have it all under control. You are going to have to trust me on this one. Besides, we have the catalogue to complete. I thought you might be rather busy.'

His hair was roughly tousled and his eyes were still a little sleepy in the warm morning sunshine which hit the south-facing patio first thing in the morning. As he smiled at her in that light, he looked ten years younger and twice as attractive. And he had *that* look she was starting to recognise so well.

Mimi looked away from him and with a gentle shake of the head started teasing away the layers of pastry from her croissant. 'You are scheming something. I can tell from your face. And I suppose you're not going to tell me about it either.' She sighed. 'I don't think my poor brain can cope with any more big surprises at this time of the morning.'

He tried to suppress a smile and the whole of his upper lip twitched and twisted in reaction.

'Then you have something to look forward to.'

Three hours later, Mimi strolled along the inner-city pavement with her head high and a fixed smile on her lips. It was almost noon on a Monday, the sun was shining and she was wearing her dove-grey trouser suit with the narrow lapels and high-waisted flat-front trousers with side pockets large enough that you could actually use them.

Hal had called her with an address and a vague promise that she was going to like the new venue. Now, that was at least some positive news she could hang on to.

As she caught her reflection in the plate glass of a shop window, she could not help but smile back in guilty pleasure. Her cream and grey, woven leather, sling-back high-heel sandals were a perfect match for her cream silk blouse. It had taken her over an hour to style her hair and make-up so that she looked as sophisticated and elegant as her clothes were designed to be but, yes, she did feel fantastic wearing a design from the Mimi Ryan New Classics collection.

And according to Helena, who was taking care of the shop, she didn't look too bad either.

Well, she had at least to *look* the part if she was going to visit a swanky London hotel, even if she did feel like all the stuffing had been teased out of her. Even after her first good night's sleep in weeks, she still felt tired, but dared not let it show. Hal had promised her an exciting venue to replace the burnt and flooded hotel. So, if there was ever one occasion when she had to make a good impression on a hotel manager, this was it.

Smart hotels rarely had function rooms large enough to stage a catwalk show, especially at short notice, so this new hotel must be quite something. Especially when Hal had kept the location secret until the very last minute. She had waited by her mobile phone on tenterhooks until he'd texted her with an address only a few minutes' walk from the original venue in this very smart part of town.

This was ever so slightly worrying!

She knew this part of London reasonably well, and she certainly could not recall another large hotel in the area, but things did change very quickly. A new hotel might welcome the publicity from a charity event.

On the other hand, Hal obviously liked playing tricks on people and giving them surprises.

What was he up to?

She was soon going to find out. This was the correct street and the... Oh, no. The Community Climbing Centre.

Climbing centre!

Oh, very funny, Hal. Very funny. Just one more excuse for him to show off his physical prowess before they headed off to the real venue.

Good joke.

Shaking her head, Mimi peeked inside the open door of the huge red-brick building. What she saw was so unlike anything she had ever seen in her life it knocked the air from her lungs.

The old factory building had been opened up to create a vast, flat, hangar-like space with high ceilings above huge stone-block walls.

And covering three of those walls were immense structures, perhaps thirty feet high or more, with small multicoloured blobs stuck all over their surfaces. Arches overhanging huge blocks, straight walls, angled walls. The sheer scale was overwhelming.

Smaller versions of the climbing walls poked up

from the floor like huge boulders which had been dropped there from space. On closer inspection, the blobs looked like half-cups or pegs. They must be where the climbers hung on to as they moved up the wall. Her high-heeled shoes made a distinctive clatter on the hard floor and the sound echoed around the huge room as she moved farther into the cavernous space.

'Hey, Mimi! I'm over here!' Hal called out, and she walked in the direction his voice had come from. She couldn't see anyone, then suddenly there was a low grunt and she looked up above her head instead of around.

Hal was hanging almost horizontal from a rope attached to a belt around his waist and a harness between his legs. He was sitting in a bucket-shaped seat being lowered to the ground by two young men who were in charge of the ropes.

Mimi's breath caught in her throat as she watched him descending down the climbing wall.

'Hal! Please be careful!'

Thirty seconds later, Hal's right foot made contact with the ground at the base of the wall; he unclipped his harness and pulled off his climbing helmet.

His face was alive with energy and excitement as he thanked the helpers then turned to Mimi.

'Welcome to my world.'

Mimi glanced back at the wall above her head and slowly exhaled.

'That was impressive. Do you come here often?'

'A couple of times a year,' he replied. 'This is where the local experts give free climbing lessons for the disabled. They love it, especially the kids. Most of the money from the fashion show is coming right here, so feel free to pop in any time you like for a bit of abseiling. That harness can take a wheelchair.'

She shook her head very slowly from side to side. 'I am far too much of a coward to even try, but thanks for the invite.'

Hal laughed and rapped his knuckles on the top of his helmet. 'Me too. It is all about controlling your fear; that's what makes climbing so safe. I've just been following up with the volunteers to check that they are okay with the new venue before Saturday, but don't worry about that. Right now I have a far more interesting job.'

Mimi rubbed her hands together in delight and positively jiggled on the spot.

'I can't wait to see this amazing venue you have found! Please tell me it's gorgeous. Please. How far is it?'

Hal grabbed his crutch, planted his other hand on his hip then looked around the room in wide-eyed surprise. 'You mean you don't like the place? The volunteers have been up since dawn cleaning it up just for you.'

Mimi's breath caught in her throat and a deep, cold pit of fear started building up in the bottom of her stomach—until she noticed that the side of Hal's mouth was twitching.

She thumped him on his shoulder with her handbag instead and scanned the huge, empty space.

'Pest. You almost had me going there for a moment. I know I like a challenge, but...'

Hal threw back his head and burst out laughing, the kind of deep belly-laugh that echoed around the room and through her bones, before he casually threw his arm around her shoulder and gave her a gentle shake.

'Got you! Not that there is anything wrong with the place. It would actually fit everything we need. But...' He smiled. 'I called an old friend last night, who called some of her friends, and after a couple of hours of overseas detective-work we managed to track down a sister of another friend whose family have just bought a luxury Edwardian hotel overlooking the park. Five minutes away on foot. Apparently it is so exclusive that they only take bookings from very special guests around certain dates. My friend managed to persuade them to squeeze us in next Saturday.'

'I don't know how you managed it, but thank you,' Mimi added with a sigh, and grinned back at him. 'Can we go there now? And please say yes.'

'I have an action plan. I have a map. I have volunteers to make it happen. Time to get this show on the road.'

Then, without asking permission or a second's delay, Hal reached out with his right hand and took firm control of her left, as though it was something he did every day of the week.

The rough skin of his fingertips brushed against the smooth skin of her palm and the shock of that simple touch rippled through her body and startled her with the intensity of the sensation.

It was as though all of Hal's strength, energy and focus were flowing down from his body into hers through the tiny area of skin-to-skin contact, thrilling her, energising and invigorating her, a cold, refreshing shower pouring new life and enthusiasm and hope into her heart.

The overwhelming sensation was so overpowering that it took a few seconds for her brain to catch up with the fact that she was holding hands with Hal Langdon.

And she liked it. She liked it more than she could put into words.

Her mother had been a natural Italian extrovert; hugging, holding and kissing were very much part of her daily life in the knitting shop with friends and family. But somehow that open need for physical connection had not been passed down to her daughter.

'Daddy's girl.' That was what her mum had liked to call her. Mimi was like him in colouring and cool intelligence with the kind of English reserve that infuriated her.

Except that right now, holding Hal's hand and feeling the power of that connection, she could not help but wonder if some of her Italian heritage had passed down to her after all. She adored it. Why had she held back for so long when it felt so good?

Or was this a lot more to do with the man who was doing the holding?

'Ready to go?' Hal asked with a smile, and gave her hand a gentle squeeze. 'It's right this way.' Then, without waiting for her reply, he meshed her fingers even tighter between his, claiming her, determined to make sure that this time they were in it together, side by side.

He took off at a blistering pace, his crutch swinging forward step by step as he blasted through the doors, head down like a bull about to charge, pulling her along with him without a dot of consideration for her heels.

She had sometimes wondered what it would be like to be tied to the tail of a comet.

Now she was in great danger of being burnt up in the heat of the flames.

CHAPTER EIGHT

IT WAS late Friday afternoon and Mimi was sitting at one of her studio tables enjoying her second cup of tea while Hal peered at the framed photographs on the kitchen wall as he slurped down his coffee. Mimi leant back against the warm cushion and closed her eyes with a contented smile.

A week ago she had been so nervous she could hardly speak. Now it was the day before the show. She had a pre-show fundraiser to go to that evening and, instead of being terrified and nervous, she felt okay.

In fact, she felt better than okay.

The past five days had passed in a whir of relentless activity and excitement.

The show catalogues had been printed on time, and even Poppy had declared that the entire collection was spectacular when she had dropped in that morning to check they were still alive and on track.

The hardest part was that every time she turned around Hal had his camera focused on her.

Apparently he needed photos of the designer at work for the promotional material on the day. The first day had been torture. She had squirmed and wriggled inside her casual sewing clothes for at least an hour until Hal had started chatting to her about the music he had picked out for the fashion show.

Devious. She should be cross with him. Except that the ruse had worked brilliantly. Somehow she had been so busy talking about their shared love of music, while her fingers had worked methodically on the fine fabrics of a blue cocktail dress she'd been making for the party, that she had completely forgotten the fact that Hal could chat with his finger pressed on the camera shutter.

Which was nothing short of a miracle.

How had he managed to spot her weakness for good music?

She had been so outraged when he'd told her about the playlist he had come up with that she had somehow forgotten he was taking her picture.

Boy bands from the 1980s were not exactly what she'd had in mind at *all*.

She had hoped the models would be walking down the catwalk to the background sound of classical music or an upbeat contemporary classic.

Okay. In a moment of weakness, she might have agreed Hal would be in charge of the music and video at the event, but that had been before she had realised he had no idea about contemporary music.

It had taken four evenings of listening after dinner to dozens of movie soundtracks and popular classical music, followed by arguing late into the night, to convince Hal that there were alternatives to big rock groups. They had spent hours sifting through her collection of music CD's and laughing over old favourites until some sort of very unusual compromise had been reached. Last night, over their red wine on the patio, they had finally come up with a great compilation sequence which was perfect for the atmosphere and the clothes.

So at least the music was sorted out.

All they had to do now was finalise the visuals and make sure everything was in place for the show tomorrow.

It was actually going to happen! And she had made it real.

'Now, who do we have here? Why, I believe it is Miss Mimi Fiorini Ryan. And what *is* she wearing? This is a future blackmail-photo if ever I saw one.'

Mimi peered at the photograph Hal was holding, pressed both hands to her glowing cheeks and groaned. 'Oh, no! My graduate fashion show. Please, put it back in the desk drawer out of sight. I am begging you. I'm still living that one down.'

'What, and miss all the fun? But you are going to have to explain the dustbins and black plastic bags.' He peered closer at the picture. 'Are those girls wearing steel-toe-capped boots?'

Minmi replied, 'The famous-name photographer was bored with slick clothing shows. So he decided to turn my theme of "working girl" into "rich city girl who wears couture when she collects refuse." Without telling me in advance!'

She shivered in horror at the memory. 'I was so naive I actually thought that I could trust my work to this man who had been taking photos for couture houses since before I was born. What made it worse, of course, was that my darling mother was so proud of my work she invited the entire Fiorini family to my graduation show. I have never been so humiliated in my life! My cousins took great delight in ridiculing me the whole way through. They particularly liked the old banana-skins and strips of toilet paper the stylist had pinned to the silk velvet evening-skirts.'

Hal peered at the tableau and gave a long whistle. 'Ouch. Still, student of the year? Special prize in tailoring? It's a good thing you're so modest, Miss Ryan. Most people would be singing these kinds of reviews from the highest rooftop.'

He lifted up his beaker of coffee and gave her a short bow. 'I had no idea I was in the presence of such a star! Many congratulations.'

She pushed out her lips. 'Well, thank you, kind sir. Not sure about the "star" bit, but I am getting there.'

Hal took another slurp of coffee in silence and gave her that certain closed-mouth smile she had become used to over the past week. His eyes were still fixed on her so intently that she lowered her drink to the table and sighed loudly.

'Okay; I'm starting to recognise that look. What have I done wrong now? Please, tell me now and be done with it. There is still a lot to do before the party tonight.'

'Drat.' He smiled. 'Am I that obvious?' His fingers ran up and down the side of the beaker. 'However I ask this it is going to sound insulting—so I am going to just ask it and be done with it. Ready?'

Mimi took a quick sip, swallowed down hard and nodded. 'As I ever will be. Go. Ask.'

'Okay. You were a star student at a famous fashion and design school. Hey—it has to be famous if I've heard of it. The clothes look terrific and you obviously have talent. So what I want to know is this: why didn't you go to work for one of the big fashion houses like Fiorini when you left college? You must have had offers. What has held you back for so long?'

What had held her back?

Hal's question echoed back at her from the quiet, calm cream walls of the studio workshop where she had spent almost every waking moment of the last ten years of her life.

Ten years of never quite knowing if the mother she had said good night to was going to be the same funny, wonderful, loving person the next morning.

Ten years of working in precious snatches of time while her mother had been sleeping or had been with one of the series of neurologists or other specialists they had seen when she had been lucid enough to recognise that there was a problem.

Her career had been built on precious stolen minutes where she could retreat inside herself to work, think and plan—perhaps two hours early in the morning, or during the night when the sleep-walking had started and she had needed to be here constantly to stop her Mum from hurting herself.

Ten years of working into the night on a distant dream of launching her own clothing range, sketch after sketch, sample after sample. Hours of detailed study so that she could become an expert in pattern cutting and tailoring, building on the skills she had learned at college.

She had not had any other choice, she had been on her own—instead of being part of a couture team that already had all of the skills and experience needed to create the best.

It had been her choice to turn down the offers. Her decision. No self-pity was allowed.

Until Hal had arrived she'd had no idea how much she'd missed working one to one with another experienced professional. The students were great, of course, but she was the course director, not their equal.

Suddenly aware that he was still staring at her as though he was trying to read her mind, Mimi made eye contact and tried to work out whether she could trust this man with the truth.

There had been so many lies and half-truths in her life, she was tired of it.

She had to decide right now whether Hal was someone who was likely to mock her and her choices, or would listen, understand and not judge. Whether she could tell him the truth and expect the same in return.

His eyes were warm and gleaming with mischief and laughter, not condemnation or criticism. He really did appear to want to know the answer to his question, but was probably determined to have some fun at her expense.

It was not Hal's fault. How could he know what she had been through?

Except that telling Hal about her Mum and her mental illness would mean exposing herself to his pity. And that was the last thing she wanted, or needed. From her neighbours and friends who had known the family for years? Yes. From Hal Langdon and trade professionals in the career she had chosen? Not so much.

He smiled at her, twinkled up his nose and scrubbed at it fiercely with the knuckle of a very grubby forefinger, spreading dust all over the end of it.

And it broke the spell.

Mimi grinned and sniffed at her own stubbornness. She had nothing to be ashamed about. On the contrary; she had come through ten years of struggle. She could cope with having some fun with a handsome man who seemed to be enjoying her company as much as she enjoyed his.

If Hal wanted to find fun in everything he did, then maybe she could try and do the same.

Which was why she sat back in her chair and waved her arm regally around the studio before replying in a sweet, jokey voice.

'You mean, what am I doing in a cosy knitting shop on a sleepy street when I could be living the high life in Paris or Milan, going to celebrity parties every night where the guests are all wearing

Mimi Ryan exclusives? Was that the kind of thing you were thinking of?'

'Absolutely,' he replied, and his eyebrows rose quizzically to match his cheeky smile. 'Wait; let me guess. You ran off to Timbuktu with a handsome goat-hair salesman and lived the desert life until he swapped you for several fine camels? Or perhaps a slick Italian carried you away to the Fiorini factory in Milan to join the family firm? No, forget that last one; far too boring. I have a feeling you spent a few years doing something far more outrageous. Am I right?'

She smiled at him and raised her tea cup. 'Spot on. I did the one thing nobody expected me to do.' Then she grinned with a wide smile. 'My mother became seriously ill and needed me to take care of her, so I stayed right here, in this shop and this studio, and built up my business empire from this very table.' She nodded at him. 'You should feel very honoured, you know. I don't allow my other fans to enter the centre of operations of my business. It is a rare event indeed.'

Mimi waited for the laughter and sarky remark, but it never came.

Instead Hal exhaled very, very slowly at her calm

and positive reply and pushed away from the table and back against his hard wooden chair. 'I'm so sorry,' he replied in a voice so crammed with emotion that Mimi fought back a comment about his sense of timekeeping and waited in silence, content to simply watch Hal and his reaction.

What had she expected—surprise? Disbelief? Ridicule, even? Whatever it had been, it had not been this. He looked totally stunned.

Hal's eyes were focused on his fingers which were still wrapped tightly around his now empty beaker, his eyebrows tight and stressed to match the tension in his face.

Well, that was a mistake, Mimi thought to herself. Time to change the subject. 'I am the one who should apologise. I didn't mean to make you feel uncomfortable or awkward. This is the end of a busy few days and we don't have much time to get ready for the party tonight. Would you like more coffee? I'll be right back.'

Only, as she tried to leave the table, Hal's fingers released the cup and meshed with hers, locking them in place in a bond so firm that she could not escape.

'Not uncomfortable; not awkward. Just stunned.

Not many people surprise me these days, Mimi. It comes as a bit of a shock to find out that there is even more behind your talent than I could have imagined.'

He was smiling at her now with a kind of smile that he had never used before. It was warm, sincere and new, and so special she was mesmerised by it.

Was this the real Hal? It was not the quiet, fierce looking version of Hal that had intimidated her the first time they met, or the bossy brother, or high flyer, or whatever other role he decided to act out. This was the real deal. The genuine true man she had only imagined before this moment.

And the real Hal Langdon was a knockout.

It was the real Hal who leant forward, lifted up her hand to his lips and kissed the back of her knuckles with such tenderness, while his brown eyes were locked onto hers, never breaking that connection as he gently lowered their linked hands back onto the table.

'If you want to talk about it, I am right here. But, if you don't, that is okay too. Either way you are right.' He nodded. 'It was a remarkably courageous thing to do.'

Mimi blushed down to the base of her neck but managed a half-smile.

'I never thought about it being courageous. Mum had her first stroke when I was in my last year at college and she never truly recovered. We were prepared for a long recovery, but not the dementia that it caused, and the other strokes that eventually took her.'

'Oh, Mimi. I am so sorry. The dementia must have been so hard.'

'The doctors did warn us. And in the end it had to be my decision. I knew what the cost would be right from the start. So did my mother. She even tried to talk me out of it when the offers from the fashion houses started to come in. She even suggested that she would sell the shop and move into a nursing home where she could have twenty-four-hour care.'

He seemed to suck in a breath, and there was a quiver around his lower lip, but before she could respond Hal recovered and lifted his chin a little to reply.

'I can understand why your Mum made that offer. She must have been a remarkable woman.'

'She was. But how could I allow her to do that?

How could I walk away and lead some glittering, high-flyer life somewhere knowing that my own mother, who had sacrificed everything for me, was sitting confused and frightened, surrounded by strangers who were simply being paid to look after her.'

Mimi's shoulders lifted up and then dropped back down.

'I couldn't do it. And I didn't *want* to do it.'

'What do you mean? It would have a lot easier on you. And would certainly have saved you a lot of pain.'

'True. But those last few years together—just the two of us, living and working in these few small rooms—were the best! I got to know my mother as my best friend before I became her full-time carer. I would not have missed that time we spent together for anything.'

Hal's fingers tightened their grip on hers to the point where they were almost hurting, and then released her so suddenly that she jolted back in startled surprise.

'I envy you that. Since my parents died there have been so many times I needed my dad. It happened so quickly. And then there was Tom...' He faltered, as though he was having trouble finding the right words. 'No; I don't know if I could have done what you did—seeing the people you know fade away and perish in front of your eyes and being powerless to do anything to help them—not sure at all. That would need a different kind of strength and courage.'

The trace of a tremor in Hal's voice and the far-away look in his eyes was almost too much for Mimi to bear. It was almost as if he was not talking about her situation at all.

They had both lost people they had loved. Perhaps that was why she had never felt connected to another person in this way before.

She was so close to tears it was embarrassing, but the old habit of keeping her feelings locked up inside still held sway and she blinked away the signs of her distress.

'It isn't easy. You're right about that.'

She paused and bit her bottom lip before looking hard into Hal's face. 'Do you mean your friend Tom Harris?'

Mimi held her breath as Hal looked away from her for a second before nodding slowly in silence. He moved just an inch or two farther away from her, and the air between them felt so fraught and tense that she rushed in to speak first. 'I'm sorry. I can only imagine how horrible the accident was. I didn't mean to pry,' she whispered. 'It's just that I don't know anything about Tom and the kind of man he was. And here I am, working to help raise funds for the charity project he started. Can you tell me something about him?'

Hal looked sideways at her and frowned. 'What do you want to know?' he replied in a low, hoarse voice.

'Oh, the crazy little details that made him your friend. What kind of pizza topping did he like? What is his house like? Did he sing out of tune? What kind of maddening habits did he have? That sort of thing.'

A deep snort and chuckle bubbled up from deep in Hal's belly and instantly Mimi felt the air thin and the mood lift.

'Chillies. He loved chillies. You know those little fiery red ones?' Hal mimed holding something between this thumb and forefinger and dropping it into his mouth. 'He could eat a whole jar all by himself then stink out the whole house for days.

And raw garlic and onion. It used to drive his girl-friend Aurelia mad.'

He lifted one hand, gestured towards the kitchen area and grinned. 'Aurelia's idea of a spicy meal is sprinkling extra cinnamon on her Danish pastry. She stayed home when we took clients to Asia, that was for sure. And, yes, come to think about it, he did sing out of tune. Especially after a long evening in the pub.

'Tom was a very special person,' Hal added with a smile, looking up at her through his long, dark eyelashes, then he took a breath. 'Actually, Aurelia has asked me to work on a documentary about Tom and his work. I'm thinking about it.' He shrugged. 'Not sure I'm ready for that yet, but who knows? Maybe one day.'

'A documentary? That would be a wonderful tribute. One thing is for sure—there is nobody else who could do it better than you. All I have is my work, which is a sort of legacy in a way. My mother had a favourite saying which used to annoy me like mad sometimes: "only forward". She would have loved to see these designs on show—so perhaps we had better get back to it.'

With that she stood up and tried to disengage

her fingers from Hal's, but he was holding them firmly enough to shift to her waist and pull her sharply towards him.

In one smooth move, Mimi was sitting on his knees with her arm around his neck, not entirely sure how she got there.

'Now, that is much better,' Hal smiled with a self-satisfied grin, his face only a few inches from hers, one arm around her waist and the other stroking the hair back from her face. 'Your mother would be proud of you. Your work is not her only legacy— she left a wonderful daughter as well.'

'Thank you, but that was far too slick! Almost as if you had done it before, hmm?' Mimi murmured as Hal's fingertips moved gently over her cheek and throat as she shuffled and twisted to get off his knees without success. His attention was totally fixed on the tiny area of her skin below each fingertip, as though it was the most fascinating thing that he had ever seen. 'You can put me down now.'

'The slickest,' Hal agreed in a low, hoarse and totally distracted voice. 'And I rather like you just where you are.'

'You have bony knees,' she complained, trying

not to close her eyes and relax into the most glorious sensation of his tender caresses.

'The boniest.'

Hal started sliding his nose into the pocket just under her ear, and suddenly Mimi could not stand it any longer. Pressing both hands flat against his chest, she pushed hard against Hal, stood up and stepped away from him, out of reach of his welcoming arms. Her heart was racing, her breathing hot, ragged and needy.

She closed her eyes for a second in the silence that followed, and did not dare open them until she had said what needed to be said.

It was so quiet he could probably hear the thumping of her heart in her chest.

This had to stop. A day from now the show would be over, Hal Langdon would be out of her life, she would be back to normal and it would be hard enough without the kind of heartbreak that Hal could bring.

No matter how much she longed to be back in his arms, she needed to distance herself from his touch that turned her resolve to jelly and that she already knew would haunt her dreams. She had spent so much time and effort protecting herself from the pain of loss and rejection she would not be able to bear it if Hal became something else she had to survive.

'It's not you. It's me. I can't do this and I'm sorry if I gave you the wrong impression. Truly sorry.'

When she dared open her eyes, Hal was on his feet. His smile had faded and been replaced with a look of concern rather than hurt, regret rather than anger.

'What are you so afraid of, Mimi? There is no shame in needing people. And I already know that there is a lot more to Mimi Ryan than I ever thought possible. Why are you so scared of letting that part of you come alive?'

'Scared? I'm scared that you will become just someone else who abandons and leaves me. Someone else I have to mourn and endure when they are gone. That is what I am scared of, Hal, and that is why I don't want you to touch me or kiss me or hold me. Can you understand that?'

Hal's gaze racked across her face for a long, searching minute as though he did not quite believe her. And, just when he opened his mouth to answer, their silent idyll was rocked by the telephone on her desk.

Neither of them moved one inch to answer it. This was too special to break off for a telephone call, and after six rings the answer machine cut in.

'Hi, Mimi, Poppy here. Hope everything is going okay. Can you do me a favour? If you see Hal can you remind him that he should have been back at my place to pick up his tuxedo half an hour ago? And we have to be there early tonight to meet and greet. Can't wait to see your outfit later. *Ciao*.'

'Your tuxedo?' Mimi said, lifting her voice a little at the end in surprise, her senses sparkling and super-sensitised to his every reaction.

He glanced down at his tatty cut-off old jeans and lifted up the hem of his T-shirt with two fingers. 'I thought this might be a little casual when I'm escorting the star of the show to her first proper fashion bash. Have to look the part for something like that.'

'You're wearing a dinner suit for me?'

'Is that so hard to believe? You deserve the best, and while I'm around that is exactly what you are going to get.' The fingers of one hand slid up into her hair and drew her closer, then closer, so that when he slanted his head and brought his warm, full lips onto hers Mimi felt weightless, her body totally supported by the ring of her arms and the buoyant life and energy in his heart.

The pressure of his moist mouth on hers increased with the heat between them. The air seemed on fire as she leant into him even more, his lips sliding back and forth, then onto her chin and throat, creating delicious shivers of heady sensation. She could have stayed there for ever in his arms, but it was Hal who moved his mouth to her forehead.

'I do understand, but I promise you that you will never need to be scared about me. I'll be back to pick you up in two hours,' he whispered in a hoarse voice. 'This is your night, Mimi. Get ready to have the time of your life!'

CHAPTER NINE

MIMI lay back against a soft duck-feather pillow on her mother's bed, her arms wrapped around a large lavender silk cushion pressed into her stomach, and smiled at the silver-framed photograph of her parents on their wedding day, their arms wrapped around each other under the glorious Italian sunshine.

Her mother was dazzlingly beautiful.

The ivory wedding dress had been designed and made by her grandmother and embellished with pearls and crystal as a labour of love by all the aunts and Fiorini workshop-ladies. The bodice and train alone had taken three weeks of painstaking hand sewing. Her father looked so proud and handsome in his best summer wool suit, fine shoes and tie. They were both so young and brimming with hope and dreams of a happy, long life together.

Mimi looked around the room and breathed in

the precious atmosphere. The scent of perfume, old wood and lavender sachets was totally unique and intense with memories.

This had been her parents' private, sacred space and the only room Mimi had not been allowed in as a child.

Of course, once her mother had become ill, all of that became unimportant. Her mother had loved Mimi to sit on her bed, laughing and chatting, huddling together, filling the room with life.

Now it seemed over-filled with wardrobes containing fifty years of memorabilia and clothes; precious, wonderful clothes: shoes, gloves, hats. A treasure trove of the beautiful things her mother had loved. Wearable art had been nothing new to Talia Fiorini Ryan.

Each week she would choose something, some treasure, to bring beauty into her life and Mimi's life. Sometimes she would wear it or display it on a dress. Other times Mimi would come back from school or university to find some jewel or exuberant hat on a box on the kitchen table. It had been her delight, and Mimi had loved her for that.

Mimi slid across the bed to sit opposite the polished cedar linen-chest with its wide, long shelves which ran along one complete wall of the bedroom. She carefully used both handles to pull out the top drawer. Her mother's wedding dress was still in its white silk bag, folded and curled around special padded sachets so that the beading would not be destroyed. Mimi ran her fingertips along the beautiful cover her grandmother had stitched and initialled by hand before closing the drawer shut with regret. It had been her mother's dream to see Mimi married in this dress. She had never got to see it.

The fact that Mimi would have had to lose several inches to actually fit into the dress was totally irrelevant. It had always been Mimi's dress. Even after all of these years, there was still the faint tang of her mother's favourite gardenia perfume. Or was she imagining it?

Sniffing back a lump in her throat, Mimi opened up the bottom drawer which held the matching silk shoes and gloves. And one more treasure—a slim shoe-box hidden from casual eyes at the back of the drawer.

Only this box did not contain shoes, but a long, dark, purple velvet bag, closed with two drawstrings. Mimi unclipped the box and the three strands of perfect creamy pearls took her breath away. The clasp was in platinum and diamonds with the mark of a famous maker, although she could barely see it through her tears.

There had been many times when selling this precious piece would have made things a lot easier, but these pearls were intended for Mimi to wear on her wedding day, and to her mother that was more important than roof repairs.

She *needed* to wear something linking her to her Mum tonight. She would be with her in spirit—that would never change—but the necklace would be a special physical connection. Not to the Fiorinis, but to the woman who had given up everything for the man she loved and the daughter she had taught so very well.

Sniffing away even more tears, Mimi slid off the bed, fastened the clasp of the pearl necklace around her neck and looked at the image which gleamed back at her from the mirror.

Wow. So this was what serious jewellery should look like. This was how designers used real jewels to turn a T-shirt and trousers into a couture outfit. She had heard about it, but until this minute she had never really appreciated it.

She *would* wear her mother's wedding pearls for the first time.

And she would wear them with love as the perfect accessory to the perfect gown.

Just like a real designer would.

Gulping down a breath and the lump in her throat, Mimi collapsed back down on the duvet and stared hard at the racks of clothes filling two wardrobes which stood opposite with their doors wide open. Clothes made by famous designers from all over Europe, including exquisite vintage Fiorini pieces made by craftswomen who had dressed royalty and famous celebrities.

As she looked at those wardrobes, wearing these fabulous pearls intended to adorn a woman accustomed to wearing couture gowns, a well of bitter doubt and fear built up in the pit of her stomach.

A real designer.

She felt as though every scrap of self-confidence and self-belief she had built up over the past few days was being sucked out of her, leaving behind an empty and self-deluded husk.

She was a total and absolute fraud. An imposter.

Mimi closed her eyes, heart thumping, her mouth dry and head aching, and snatched up the cushion, squeezing it with all her might as she tried to fight off the growing sense of panic which was threatening to overwhelm her.

Who was she trying to fool?

Whatever she did, she already knew she would be totally intimidated by the people in the room tonight.

What had she been thinking to imagine for one moment that she could launch her own range of clothing and compete against these famous names in the fashion world?

The stunning models with their perfect figures, she could cope with. It was their job to look good and they worked hard to keep it that way. But the designers, their assistants and their stylists would all be there. Experts. Trained and experienced in top design-houses.

While she was—what? What credentials did she have to offer?

She could just imagine the small talk.

And where is your salon, my dear?

Oh, I have a knitting shop in north London. Do you know the area?

Mimi groaned and pulled the cushion over her head.

What was she going to do?

Peeking over the top of the cushion, she looked at the blue cocktail dress hanging on the rail ready and waiting for her to slip on.

She had made it herself, sewn every stitch by hand. Chosen the fabric and experimented with the design for days until she was happy that it was perfect.

Looking at it now, she saw the dress through an outsider's eyes.

And was totally disgusted. It was pathetic; plain, small-town; home-made, rather than designer hand-sewn; without verve or panache. Worse, the dress was hanging next to her mother's collection of designer gowns; the comparison was so painful that she turned her head away with a shudder. She couldn't even look at the dress she had been so proud of only a few hours earlier.

If she wore that blue dress tonight, she would just be setting herself up to be the laughing stock of the show. A real country bumpkin with delusions of grandeur—just as her Fiorini cousins had said that she was. And this pearl necklace would make the contrast scream out even louder.

She was going to let Hal and Poppy down. She just knew it.

Hal had worked so hard to make her dream come true and now she was going to ruin everything.

Oh, Mum. What have I got myself into? What do I do now?

Hal Langdon swung his heavy left leg onto the top flight of steps to Mimi's apartment, let his cane take the weight and straightened his bow tie one-handed in his reflection in the glass.

He had made it; stormed the castle on his own two feet. Well, one good foot and one painful and swollen foot, but he was here all the same. The cane was a last-minute replacement for the crutch but it seemed to be working.

Not bad, mate; not bad at all. Just the right amount of style and dash to wow the fashionista into opening up their cheque books for the charity.

He stretched out his hand to ring the door-bell, then hesitated and took a breath as his hand dropped away.

Maybe this was not such a good idea after all.

Working with Mimi had given him some sense of purpose in the dark days when there had been so little light on the horizon, and he was more grateful than she could know. But it was more than that. *A lot more.*

In a few short days Mimi had become a very important part of his life.

He had never planned to need to be with her, hold her, share his life and past with her.

It had been a very long time since he had felt so close to a girl and the impact had sent him reeling.

Only a few hours ago she had also shared some of the pain of the last twelve months with him. She had trusted him with a part of her life which was so very personal.

He had been totally in awe. For a few minutes, holding her in his arms, he had come so close to telling her what had happened on the mountain that day. So very close. But his nerve had faltered and he had lost that tiny door into his heart that only Mimi seemed able to open. Her pain had been so raw and fresh; he had no right to add fuel to that fire with his own pain.

Mimi had had to watch her mother fade over months and years of extended suffering. The fire of life and power that had been Tom Harris had been extinguished in a fraction of a second when his head had hit the rocks. How could he compare her pain to his?

That would have been totally unfair on both of them. But at that moment something had changed for him.

His admiration and respect for her had moved into a new depth. A depth which had startled him then and was still singing in his head even now.

What he was feeling for Mimi Ryan was something unique and precious. And he had no clue about where it was going to take them.

She had a life here, a home, a business and a career she had built up at huge personal cost. Her gentle touch had told him that perhaps, just perhaps, there might be a place for him in her life. Perhaps even a place to come back to. A centre around which the turmoil of his life could move when he was ready to work and rediscover where he fitted into this crazy world.

But in the meantime he had one mission alone: to help Mimi Ryan celebrate the launch of her clothing collection and the work she had done for Tom's project.

And he had every intention of seeing that mission through to the end.

His finger pressed on her doorbell; a very strange version of Vivaldi, played on an out-of-tune piano and a tin whistle, filled the calm evening. It was certainly a door chime with a difference.

A few seconds later he heard a strange shuffling sound and the door opened.

To reveal not quite the vision of loveliness that he had been expecting.

Mimi was wearing a long towelling dressing gown tied tight around her waist. The normally luscious hair was swept back from her forehead by a headband made from what looked like a knitted tie, exposing a pale and exhausted-looking face.

Her face and neck were red, her eyes were puffy, and from the state of the smudged mascara all over her eyelids she had started on the make-up and given up halfway through.

Okay...

'Ready to go to the ball, Miss Ryan?' Hal asked in the most positive, energetic and enthusiastic voice he could come up with. 'Love the outfit, by the way. So different! Glass slippers are optional.' And he glanced at her feet.

Mimi looked down. She was still wearing pink fluffy slippers with bunny ears. 'Oh,' she replied in a dazed voice, and blinked several times. 'Is it that time already?' She glanced at the kitchen wall-clock and groaned. 'And now I am going to be late as well.' Her shoulders slumped even lower and she held the door open for Hal. 'You had better come in. I'm having a bit of a problem.'

'So I see. Anything I can help you with?'

Her answer was a quick nod. Then she did something quite extraordinary.

She held out her hand towards him as though she needed him.

She needed him.

Hal grasped his cane even tighter, took her tiny fingers in his right hand and smiled weakly at her, willing any strength he had to pass through that tenuous connection to soothe what was troubling her. Because something had obviously happened to upset her, and for once he was going to keep quiet until she was ready to tell him.

He held on to Mimi's hand as she drew him across the kitchen and into a large old-fashioned bedroom filled with heavy wooden furniture: wardrobes, chests, a dressing table, and one huge bed with an elaborate polished headboard.

Every flat surface in the room seemed to be

covered with photographs, shoes or clothing of all kinds and shapes and colours. Bags and shoes were scattered all over the carpet between the open wardrobes and the bed.

If this bedroom was anything to go by, the girl was out of control and floundering.

Mimi collapsed down on the soft bedspread and he shuffled along to sit next to her. Her fingers slipped from his grasp so that she could steady herself. There was a man's jacket draped along the pillow next to a very flimsy coffee-coloured lacy garment, but he said nothing.

The moment he moved his arm around the place on her huge dressing gown where her waist should be, Mimi leant her body against his so that her head could rest on his right shoulder.

He closed his eyes and held her closer, his chin resting gently on her head, breathing in the scent of her perfume and her, listening to the soaring classical music which was playing somewhere in the flat. Seconds. Minutes. His body was reacting in ways he didn't want it to, but he couldn't risk losing her by rushing her. Not now. She was too important to him to mess it up with motivational speeches, or by challenging her to argue with him, and break her out of whatever slump she was in.

'Do you realise that this is our first anniversary?' Hal whispered into the air above her head. 'This time last week I was making you spill your coffee onto your shoe. Have you forgiven me for that yet, by the way?'

The girl below his chin sniffed and replied in a trembling voice, 'Not a bit.'

Hal smiled to himself. The old Mimi was still in there.

'Drat. I was hoping I had redeemed myself along the way.'

Mimi instantly twisted around inside the circle of his arm and lifted her hand to press against his cheek so tenderly and with such exquisite feeling that, looking into her eyes, Hal felt his heart melt with the sight of her need and pain. With that came a feeling and connection with her that was so new, so raw and so intense that he was speechless and powerless against the force of it.

'You *have* redeemed yourself, in so many ways. Don't you dare think any differently.'

He smiled, took both of her hands in his and held them tight against his chest, before daring to lock his eyes onto hers and whisper, 'Then tell me what has upset you so much. Trust me. It's okay.'

Mimi spoke with a gentle nod. 'I was going to use one of Mum's evening bags tonight. And I found this inside.'

She slid one of her hands out from Hal's, drew a small snapshot of a slim, handsome man from her dressing-gown pocket and passed it to him. Hal glanced at the man in the photograph, looking for the clues that would tell him why she was so distraught. He was dark-haired with green eyes and was wearing the jacket lying on the bed.

'It's my dad. Mum ordered that jacket for him about a year before he died,' Mimi told him as she dropped her forehead onto Hal's shoulder.

'I didn't even know she had kept the jacket until I started looking for something to wear tonight which I might vaguely squeeze into.'

Mimi looked down at the photograph and stroked the crinkled, well-faded print.

'As far as my mother's family were concerned, my father was an outsider, you see. An outsider who was never going to be allowed to become a part of the Fiorini company, no matter how skilled and successful he was. And Mum didn't see that until it was too late.'

Her head lifted and she stroked the hair back over Hal's ears absentmindedly as her fingers lovingly caressed his scalp. 'My mother spent years moving back and forwards between here and Milan. Sometimes she would be gone for a few weeks, then home for maybe a couple of months, but there would be another crisis and she would be called back. And she went; every single time. Because they were her family and she loved them.'

Her fingers slid lower until she was holding his face in her hands and her forehead was pressed against Hal's, her breath warm on his skin.

'But they didn't love her enough to find room for my father. It was February, it was winter in the Alps, and he crashed on the way to bring her home to London. He died; he died, Hal. Trying to bring her home to be with me.'

Hal kissed the top of her head and stroked her hair before speaking.

'I am so sorry. Did they try and make her move back to live there after he died? In Milan?'

Mimi nodded. 'Of course. But Mum was in a terrible state and blamed them all for what had happened. The screaming and shouting went on for weeks. So we brought him home and we stayed here. And she never went back.'

Mimi pulled gently away from Hal and she reached up and stroked his face and tried to smile. 'Seeing this photograph again out of the blue like this brought back all of the pain and the bitterness I felt back then; the accusations. The terrible things they said about the pathetic life she had made with her fat, ugly carthorse of a daughter and her loser husband.'

She raised her head and smiled at Hal who had hissed and stiffened his back in response to what she had told him.

Mimi looked up into his eyes. 'It's okay. I came to terms with how I looked a long time ago. My mum was so pretty, elegant and petite—but she was also a very clever woman. She made her own decisions. She could have said no to her family, but she didn't. She wanted to be there. She loved her old life of luxury and wealth.'

She swallowed down hard but did not break eye contact. 'Don't you see? That was why she came back to wallow in the guilt of my father's death. It was to punish herself! And the only way she could do that was to break any contact with the family and pretend they were the source of our problems.'

Hal wrapped his arm around her and held her tight as Mimi whispered the words into his shoulder. 'Do you know the worst thing? I didn't realise that until tonight. Just sitting here going through the clothes, then finding the jacket and the photo, it all just clicked into place and I finally understood the truth. And it is just so very sad, for all of us.'

'You're right,' he replied. 'That is sad.'

Hal held her in silence for a few seconds until an ornate mantle-clock sounded out the hour.

They were going to be late for their own party. And there was a car outside with the engine running, expecting Hal and his date to emerge any minute.

His brain processed his options at lightning speed. There was no way that he could leave Mimi like this. He had committed to making this fundraiser the best it could be, but if Mimi needed him to stay with her then that was what he had to do.

He blinked several times as the implications hit home.

Somehow over the past week Mimi Ryan had become a lot more important to him than the goal he had thought was the only thing that mattered. His driving ambition to make the show a success for Tom and the project he had started had been fuelled by his guilt and obligation. Only somewhere along the way Mimi had changed him.

Sitting here now, holding this amazing woman in his arms, he knew that he only had one goal which truly mattered: making Mimi happy. The charity and the show were secondary. And, strangely enough, he liked the idea. He liked it a lot.

CHAPTER TEN

'TELL me what you want to do,' Hal said, speaking into her hair. 'I am happy to stay right here if you don't feel up to going out, but I have to tell you something: if we stay on this bed for much longer, your dad's jacket is going to get very creased.'

Mimi's face broke into something close to a grin, and Hal used his thumb to wipe away the last remnants of tears from her cheek.

'Poppy would kill us if we didn't turn up for the fundraising party, after all the trouble she has gone to in setting it up. And I suppose we are the stars of the show,' Mimi replied with a thin smile.

Hal pushed his lips out in agreement. 'That is a distinct possibility, I have to admit, but it would be worth it.' His hands gently slid the knitted hairband down over the back of her head and dropped it on the bedcover. 'If it gave me the chance to prove to you what a beautiful and truly amazing woman you are.'

His reward was a knockout smile that sent him spinning. He squeezed her waist a little firmer and felt something rigid pressing back at him.

In an instant he was tugging at her dressing gown and trying to peer down the gap.

'What *are* you wearing under that less-than-attractive garment? No offence, but it feels like body armour!'

Mimi chuckled and paused for a second before slowly untying the belt of her dressing gown.

'You mustn't laugh,' she said with a sigh. 'I was trying to get into one of my mum's lovely dresses, but I almost burst the seams and ruined it. They were made to measure for a woman several inches shorter, and smaller where it matters. So it was time to take drastic measures.'

She slid the dressing gown at the back to reveal a pretty lilac corset—or rather most of it. The back seemed to be gaping open, and he sucked in a breath to help steady the sudden increase in temperature in the room when he caught sight of her bare back.

Her shoulders came up into a shrug as she pulled the dressing gown back into place and her lips quivered as she tried to smile at him. 'Yet another reason to feel fat and frumpy. I can't even close the zip on my old corset, never mind fit into one of her gowns! And, now the zip is stuck, I can't even get out of the thing.'

She looked down at her hands and shook her head. 'I have nothing to wear to go to the ball, and a day suit would be totally wrong. So, unless you have a fairy godmother handy, perhaps you should go on your own and send my apologies. I'll be fine here; really! Just fine.'

'A corset? You were trying to get into a corset so you could fit into a dress several sizes too small for you?' Hal sighed for a moment, horrified at the very idea that Mimi thought that she was overweight and unattractive, and his connection moved to another level.

'Do not mock. This is what girls do,' Mimi replied, squirming on the bed.

'Well, this is what boys do.'

Hal grabbed hold of his cane and pushed himself off the bed. Turning back to Mimi, he extended his right hand palm-up and, curling his fingers, took her hand in his.

'Your dressing table awaits, my lady.' He bent down and whispered in her ear. 'You need to get out of that corset. I have some experience in un-zipping zips—and, before you go there, please remember that I occasionally share a flat with Poppy and her roommates and have done for several years. I am therefore familiar with various types of zips, and lacings, buttons and every other sort of fastening. In all kinds of interesting places. It is amazing how creative fashion photographers have to be these days.'

Pushing back his shoulders and slipping off his dinner jacket, Hal propped his cane on the bed, steadied himself against her chair and rubbed both hands together. He winked at Mimi as she looked back at him in the mirror on the dressing table. Her eyes were wide. Amazing. Tantalising.

She did not know what he planned to do but she was going to have to trust him anyway.

His heart sang. He had been right to ring her doorbell after all. And this was one Cinderella who was definitely going to the ball.

'I have warm hands, and can close my eyes

if you need me to, but that dressing gown is coming off.'

Mimi was biting her lower lip when he checked the mirror, and he smiled at her with raised eyebrows. Then she lowered her hands to the belt and released it little by little so that Hal could help her shrug the fabric down below her waist, exposing the top of her burgundy lace panties.

'Now, that is a lot better,' he groaned between his teeth. 'The pearl necklace is a particularly classy touch. And you have great taste in lingerie, young lady.'

Mimi's face had turned several shades of scarlet but she managed to mouth a 'thank you' between her blushes as Hal moved closer into her body. His weight shifted onto his good leg so that his hands could massage the stress out of her shoulders, before running down the centre of her back towards the top of her corset.

She was tensing up. Little wonder, considering what she was almost wearing. A thin layer of silk separated her sumptuous skin from his fingertips and he was trying with all his might to forget that fact.

'It does make me wonder why you don't want to

wear your own designs,' Hal said as he felt some of
the tension ease away under his strong fingertips.
'You have some beautiful evening gowns in your
collection.'

She looked back at him from the mirror for a
second before replying, 'I just don't have the experience or training the other designers have, Hal.
I just know that I am going to humiliate myself—
and you and Poppy in the process. It would be a lot
better for the fundraiser if I didn't go at all tonight.'

Hal moved his right hand down Mimi's back
and slowly released the zipper from where it had
become snagged. Only he had to slide the fingers
of his left hand under the fabric and onto her warm
skin to do so. He felt the thump-thump of Mimi's
heart rate increase, at the same time as his own,
at the shock of the sensation of skin against skin.

He slowly, slowly drew the zipper down the back
of the corset until both sides were released. Only
he did not let her go, but slid his fingers forward
under the boned corset. His mouth moved against
the right side of her neck as each hand circled the
skin around her waist, releasing the fabric away
from her body, moving in gentle caresses as he
did so.

'Go on,' he whispered as she arched her neck back against his chest. 'Tell me what's changed. You were so confident this morning.'

'I made the mistake of comparing my work against my family's heritage.' Mimi breathed in hot short breaths as her body swayed under his hands, her hands still pressing the corset bodice against her bosom. 'And I don't even come close to that level of craftsmanship.'

'You are just as talented,' Hal said as he started to kiss her ear before moving onto her throat, lifting up the pearl necklace with his chin and nuzzling underneath.

'Hmm? Not so sure about that.' Mimi tried to turn around but Hal turned up the heat, gliding his hands up and down her ribcage. Then his hands stilled, resting lightly on her waist as she held the front of her corset against her breasts.

'Look at the girl in the mirror—the one in front of you right now,' Hal murmured, his breath hot on her neck as his body pressed even closer to hers. He leant his chin on her naked shoulder so that he could look into the mirror at the same time as she did. 'The girl I am looking at is beautiful, talented, funny and clever and so very, very attractive.'

She tried to answer but he shushed her. 'This is why I am going to fight every manly instinct to lock the door and wreck your bed. Instead, I shall make the ultimate sacrifice and take you to the party tonight, wearing that blue dress you created, so that I can show you off as my date.'

He smiled at her reflection. 'Now, you don't get much bigger sacrifices than that! Have faith in me; I'll take care of you. And you are *not* going to be humiliated. Okay?'

Mimi turned her head around so she could smile into those deep caramel eyes as Hal lifted a wisp of hair away from her face.

'That blue dress? The one hanging up over there which I rejected three hours ago? And you are going to take care of me?'

'That blue dress. Although…'

'Although?' Mimi asked, her eyes still lost in his.

'Those pearls are amazing, but I still think you are missing one last thing to make your outfit complete, Miss Ryan,' Hal said, and reached inside the pocket of his trousers. 'I'm sorry if it got a little crushed on the way, but it is our first anniversary, after all.'

Mimi looked down at the velvet box Hal was holding out to her and breathed in.

'I didn't expect a present. Thank you, but you shouldn't have. I...' Then he opened the box. And there was the most stunning, perfect brooch she had ever seen in her life: a cluster of garnets had been formed in a silver metal into a flower vase. And in each of the three channels had been threaded a crimson-red, living rosebud. As he lifted it towards her, the scent of the roses seemed to fill the space between them. She had never seen anything like it.

'May I?' Hal asked. Mimi could only nod as he stepped back, slipped the blue silk chiffon cocktail dress from its hanger and draped it in front of Mimi so that she could hold it against her body on top of the corset.

His smooth fingertips gently caressed the upper outline of her breast before swiftly piercing the chiffon, fastening the pin and locking it in place.

Mimi stared in amazement at her reflection in the mirror. He was right; the blue dress was perfect. The pearls and the garnet brooch should not have worked together, but they did. And it was exactly what she needed. He stood behind her, his head on her shoulder, arms clasped around her waist. It was one of those precious moments she wished would go on for ever.

'How did you know?' she eventually asked in a whisper. Hal released her and stroked her hair between his fingers.

'Only garnets will work with this hair. Beautiful. And so are you,' Hal replied, and then saw the time on his watch. 'And you are going to be very late for your own party, and Poppy's spies are going to report back that I held you up. Shall we go? Make our entrance? I only hope someone has a camera good enough to capture how stunning you look.'

'Only if you promise to hold my hand, all the way, and not let go until *everybody* has seen us.' Mimi grinned as she turned to very gently graze her lips against his.

'At this precise moment, I'll promise you anything you want,' Hal said as she released him and headed towards the door. 'You look amazing. Simply stunning. That colour is... Wow.'

She could not help but laugh back at him.

'You're forgiven. And you don't look too bad yourself,' Mimi added with a nod of appreciation.

Hal gave her one fleeting kiss. 'You have ten

minutes to get ready to go to the ball. Your carriage awaits. I just hope it doesn't turn back into a pumpkin by the time we get there.'

Hal was joking about the pumpkin.

But not the ten minutes.

Mimi barely had time to wash, apply a slick of make-up and throw a lipstick and hairbrush into one of her mother's evening bags before Hal grabbed her hand firmly in his and whisked her out of the apartment and into the back seat of a luxurious chauffeur-driven car, courtesy of Langdon Events.

Luckily, the speed with which she was able to descend the stairs down from her apartment in her amazingly beautiful but impossible-to-walk-in sandals just about matched Hal's one-foot-at-a-time gait, so they were able to cling onto one other, laughing all the way down.

It was Hal who wrapped a Fiorini short swing jacket over her shoulders at the very last minute as they left. He must have searched through every garment in her mother's wardrobe while she was in the bathroom to find a large midnight-blue opera jacket that was a perfect match to her own dress—and which she could fit into with ease.

It was a magical touch she had not even thought of and would have rejected as being too Fiorini and not enough Ryan—but with the rest of the outfit…

And with Hal by her side…

It was *perfect. He* was perfect.

It was Hal who opened her car door and handed her out onto the pavement outside a stunning London hotel that Poppy had secured for the celebrity party.

Mimi had no need of a red carpet or flashing cameras and screaming fans. She was already walking on air.

It was Hal who pointed out her reflection in the floor-length mirrors as they walked hand in hand and step by slow step up the spectacular circular staircase to the party room on the first floor, and winked in appreciation as she grinned and slunk tighter against his side.

And it was Hal who whispered how beautiful she looked, and made her giggle with pleasure just as they walked into the room, so that everyone within a ten-yard radius turned around to look at them as they waltzed in hand in hand.

It was Hal who she clutched tight hold of as he guided them haltingly through the clusters of people of all shapes and sizes who had packed the room. Mimi recognised some of the mountaineers who had volunteered at the indoor climbing wall, and greeted them with a wave. Many of the guests were in day clothes, obviously just come from their work place, yet they did not seem in the least intimidated or embarrassed by being surrounded by other men and women in dinner suits and elegant evening-wear. She envied them that casual demeanour and self-confidence, yet some of it was rubbing off on her.

She had imagined that she would feel nervous and even intimidated by the stunning models Poppy had asked to support the fundraiser. But she wasn't. She felt wonderful; confident and relaxed. Delighted to be at the party to celebrate what she had achieved and raise money for the charity at the same time.

Perhaps that had a lot to do with the man whose arm she was holding on to.

Hal had told her that she was talented, pretty and attractive. And she was starting to believe him.

Something close to happiness bubbled up inside her. He was right; this should be one of the happiest evenings of her career.

By this time tomorrow evening, her very first catwalk show would be over. And she *did* deserve to feel good about that, no matter how the collection was received.

She *should* feel happy. It had taken her so many years to reach this point it was hard to believe she had done it.

He must have read her mind, for at that precise moment Hal passed her a glass of pink champagne from a silver tray a waiter was holding in front of her and smiled down at her. 'Glad you came?'

She raised her glass in a toast, took a long sip of the delicious, chilled sparkling wine and wiggled her shoulders in delight. 'I love it, Hal. I am so excited I can hardly speak. Thank you for making me change my mind about turning up.'

She stood on tiptoe, wrapped her free arm around Hal's neck and kissed him on the lips with all of the thanks and love she could come up with.

His arm circled her waist. 'Well, I am going to have to bring you to parties a lot more often if that is the kind of response I can expect. So, you are enjoying yourself?'

'Very much,' Mimi whispered in a hoarse voice, too emotional and happy to feel pathetic about almost having missed out. She hugged Hal tighter, eyes closed. As she opened her eyes and looked over Hal's shoulder, she saw Poppy waving at her from the bar, where one of the volunteers was lifting his hand jerkily, as though downing a pint glass of beer, and hanging his tongue out.

'Sorry to be a killjoy but I think the guys need that drink you promised them. Go; don't worry. I'll be right here when you get back.'

Hal's lips touched her forehead as she stood back and released him from her arms, her feet once again in contact with the soles of her evening sandals.

'Try and keep me away,' he replied, and touched the tip of her nose with his finger.

Mimi watched him stride out across the crowded room, his lopsided body moving with energy and determination. A man on a mission, driven, passionate and single-minded—even if his ankle was wrapped in a strange-looking inflatable boot and he was using a cane to propel himself along. He was unstoppable.

And she loved him for that.

Her fingers shot up to cover her mouth and she glanced from side to side to check if she had actually said that out loud, and if someone had heard her.

She loved him.

She was in love with Hal Langdon.

Bubbles of crazy joy burst inside her head and her fingers pressed even harder onto her mouth. The lip gloss was history.

Her heart was beating so fast she felt dizzy for a moment and she sipped her cool champagne, the glass trembling in her fingers.

She was in love and it was the most glorious sensation in the world.

Tomorrow she was launching her own line of clothing, she was at a fabulous party buzzing with laughter and life and energy—and she was in love with a man who thought she was beautiful and talented.

She took another sip of the delicious wine and smiled. This was turning out to be quite a party!

The fingers of her left hand touched the strand of pearls around her neck.

Only forward, Mum. Only forward.

'Oh, what a stunning jacket. It's a vintage Fiorini, isn't it?'

The sweet American voice came from behind

Mimi and she turned to face one of the loveliest women she had ever seen in her life smiling down at her. She must have been at least six feet tall, even without her four-inch heels. Long, shiny ash-blond hair was piled on top of her head in a knot then fell like a waterfall down a long and very slender back. She was the epitome of elegance and perfect grooming, the kind of girl that made Mimi want to slink into the ladies' room, repair the damage to her lipstick and start a crash diet—right now!

'Yes, it is.' Mimi laughed in surprise. Then she did a double take, her eyes wide. The blonde was wearing a Fiorini cocktail dress she had never seen outside a sketch and photographs.

'Wow. I didn't think there were any of the original Greek goddess dresses left. Fiorini couture, 1980; private clients only. How on earth did you manage to get hold of one? And it looks fantastic on you!'

The blonde's blue eyes widened and she blinked several times before blowing out hard.

'Well, thank you. You are very kind. But you have to be the first person who knew the maker, the range and the year. I am seriously impressed. You have to be another Fiorini fan. Right?'

Mimi laughed away her nervousness. 'Does it show? You might almost say that I grew up surrounded by Fiorini couture.' Instinctively her fingers pressed against the pearls around her neck for a fraction of a second before sliding to the silk. 'The jacket was made for my late mother in the '80s.'

'Oh, how fantastic!' Aurelia placed her hand over her heart and fluttered her fingers several times. 'I worked for the Fiorini family during their very last season before they sold the company. It was the finest fashion show I ever did. In fact, that is where I met Poppy Langdon. She was only seventeen at the time, and we were at the same modelling agency in London. We've been friends ever since.'

'You were a Fiorini model? Oh, now that *is* fantastic,' Mimi replied, sucking in air between her teeth to boost her courage in the presence of such a lovely woman. She stretched out her hand with such confidence that it surprised her. 'Mimi Ryan. Newbie designer and not-so-newbie knitting-shop owner. Pleased to meet you. I'm the brave soul who will be showing my new collection at the catwalk show tomorrow.'

The blonde gave her a dazzling white smile which left Mimi feeling even more in awe and shook her hand more firmly than Mimi had anticipated. 'Aurelia DiMarco. Former model, hotel owner and avid collector of anything Fiorini. And good on you for supporting the Tom Harris Foundation. You couldn't have chosen a better cause.'

'Lovely to meet you, Aurelia. And it is my pleasure…' The words dried up in Mimi's mouth as her heart leapt into her chest.

Aurelia. Tom Harris's girlfriend was called Aurelia. This had to be more than a coincidence. Oh, no. *The poor girl.* This must be a terrible ordeal for her.

The smile faltered on the lovely woman's face. 'Yes,' she nodded. 'I am *that* Aurelia. And it's okay; you don't need to be embarrassed. I'm proud of the work that Tom started. The weird thing is, if it hadn't been for that Fiorini show, I might never have met Poppy or her brother.'

Mimi's breath caught in her chest. Speaking was suddenly rather difficult.

'Her brother? Do you mean Hal? Hal Langdon?'

Aurelia raised her head and looked around the room. 'Sure. Hal was the person who introduced me to his best friend in the world, Tom Harris, mountaineer extraordinaire. He is the reason I gave up my modelling career and moved to a tiny chalet in the Alps. Oh, yes, Hal Langdon certainly has a lot to answer for!'

CHAPTER ELEVEN

AURELIA added with a sigh, 'He certainly made up for it after the accident. Hal was quite remarkable, you know. I really don't know if Tom's family or I could have coped without Hal's strength. He must have been in considerable pain those terrible first weeks but he never complained about his leg. Not once. We needed him and he was there, even though he was laid up in hospital most of the time.'

She smiled down at Mimi. 'Tom told me so many times that Hal was more like the kid brother he would have loved than an old college-pal. They really were two of a kind, always trying to push the boundaries. Life was certainly never boring when Tom and Hal got together.'

Aurelia looked out over the heads of the other guests back to the bar, where Hal and Poppy were chatting away to the crowds of people as they collected drinks. 'He must miss Tom almost as much as I do,' she added in a low, wistful voice that only Mimi would be able to hear.

Before Mimi could reply and ask her to explain, Aurelia rested her hand lightly on Mimi's arm, which had the elegant people surrounding them raising their eyebrows with more than a little envy.

'And here I am blabbering on. I've bored you for far too long. Ignore me. I knew the kind of man I was getting involved with right from the start, and I'll have plenty of time to talk to Hal over the next few days. Now,' she said firmly, linking her arm through Mimi's, 'time to show me that catalogue of your designs. I want to see everything. This show is just going to be spectacular and raise lots of cash for the foundation!'

Hal heard a sudden ripple of applause from the hotel entrance just as he was passing Poppy her chilled sparkling water. Peering out between the shoulders of the other guests, who had turned their heads to see what was happening, Hal turned to Poppy with a frown and asked, 'What's all the excitement about?'

Poppy took a long swig of her water before grinning at Hal. 'Looks like our guest of honour has arrived.' She sighed in delight. 'It's not every day that Luca Fiorini himself finds time to come to a charity event like this.'

Poppy squeezed her eyes half-shut and grabbed Hal's arm so that she could whisper, 'I was beginning to think I was never going to change Luca's mind. I have been trying to speak to his office for months and never got past his secretary. It was strange, actually. The day after I sent Luca a copy of the show catalogue, his secretary called to say that he would find the time. Ticket sales have doubled since word got out that Luca was supporting the show! It's fantastic.'

Then she stepped back and her smile faded. 'Hal? What's wrong? You look a bit pale.'

Hal lifted his chin and blew out hard. 'You invited Luca Fiorini to this party? And he only accepted when he saw the catalogue with Mimi's photograph on the back? Does Mimi know anything about this?'

'Mimi?' Poppy asked in surprise. 'No, I haven't said a thing to Mimi, but I just know that she will be thrilled! She could not ask for better publicity. Luca is giving her debut collection the Fiorini seal of approval; it's the best opportunity she could have asked for. Unless, of course, there is something that you are not telling me. Hal? What's going on?'

'I'll explain everything later, but right now I need to find Mimi before she sees who has just walked in. And fast.'

Aurelia had attracted quite an entourage of adoring fans as she wound her way into the side room set aside for the press, introducing Mimi to everyone on the way.

Within minutes Mimi found herself inundated with requests for more information, prices and delivery dates on everything in her printed catalogue.

Business cards and telephone numbers were thrust into her hands at the same rate as digital cameras were produced. Suddenly it seemed that everyone wanted to have their photograph taken with Aurelia and this cool new designer who everyone was buzzing about.

Mimi probably had more photographs taken in ten minutes than she'd had in the last ten years. But tonight, and for this wonderful opportunity, she was prepared to smile into the camera lens and pretend that she had been wrapping her arms around celebrity models all her life.

As an added advantage, her new friend provided

the perfect distraction from brooding about this new information about Hal.

She could hardly tell Aurelia that Hal had not told her anything about Tom or the accident. At least, not without looking like a complete fool. But, thinking back over the past few days, he had barely mentioned the accident at all.

Perhaps Aurelia was right and Hal was a lot more traumatised than she had thought.

The more she thought about it, the more she realised that *she* had been the one sharing her personal history with *him*. Hal had told her almost nothing about himself over these last few days that they had shared together.

Doubts niggled at the edge of her mind and threatened to undercut her new-found happiness in the way she felt about Hal. How much did she truly know about Hal's past?

How could she care so much about a man she hardly knew?

Suddenly she doubted herself and her feelings. Was this love or was she simply a lonely girl who had been forced to spend time working with an attractive man who seemed to like her in return? Little wonder that she should have a crush on him.

The smile fell from Mimi's lips as the reality of their situation started to hit home.

Hal probably spent more time in international airports around the world than camping out at Poppy's flat or her ground-floor studio. She knew that he had rented out his house in France, and London was only ever a temporary base he used when passing through, but he hadn't talked about his plans going forward.

Her life and work was built around the studio in London where she had lived all of her life. Could she move and still work the way she wanted? Probably not. And what would happen to her shop and business?

What an idiot she was to even imagine that they could have a future together. It had been fun—he had been fun—but she had better come to terms with the fact that after the show Hal would be saying his goodbyes and moving on to his next project.

And she would be back in her studio.

Someone nudged Mimi out of her thoughts and she looked up to see Aurelia and her fans jostling their way back into the main party area. A wave of warm applause, fierce whispering and laughter rolled back from the centre of the room and the guests seemed to turn towards the slightly raised podium at the front.

As Mimi stood on tip toe, Poppy shuffled forward and tapped twice on the side of a fixed microphone to attract everyone's attention before looking out over the audience and speaking in a light, clear voice.

'Ladies and gentlemen. Thank you all for coming this evening and for your support of the Tom Harris Foundation for Climbing for the Disabled. I know from personal experience that the team of volunteers do amazing work, and most of them are over there at the bar if you want to buy them a drink or write them a cheque.'

There was a round of applause from the guys, and much laughter from the guests, and Poppy waited a few seconds before speaking again. 'I am delighted to tell you that, together with our celebrity guests and fashion professionals, we have a very special guest with us tonight who has taken time out of his busy schedule to support our event.'

She paused just long enough for the room to buzz. 'Here is a man whose name speaks for itself.

Ladies and gentlemen, please welcome Mr Luca Fiorini of Fiorini International!'

Mimi's legs gave way under her just as the thunderous applause and shouting started. Sitting on the edge of the press-release table might not have been the most glamorous thing to do, but the alternative was the floor.

Luca Fiorini? *Her cousin Luca was here as a special guest?*

No. Not possible. This could *not* be happening.

Mimi leant forward and dropped her head lower to stop herself from hyperventilating and passing out. Suddenly there was no air in this room.

She had to get out of here before her cousin Luca spotted her and let the cat out of the bag.

Pushing herself to her feet was the hardest part. Creeping around the back of the party, her back to the wall while everyone was focused on the front of the room, turned out to be surprisingly easy.

Her good luck ran out within sight of the door and she was trapped in a group of new arrivals who surged into the room carrying her along with them to face the stage.

An immaculately groomed young man in a sleek, sophisticated business suit had taken over the podium, confident, tanned, elegant and commanding. Her cousin Luca. He looked like he had just landed from Planet Slick.

'Thank you for your warm welcome. I am grateful to Langdon Events for inviting me here tonight. I am honoured to support this excellent charity and look forward to being part of the celebration of fashion tomorrow.'

He lifted his chin and smiled out into the crowd like an ancient-Roman emperor deciding who lived or died in the arena. Luca knew he held the attention of the whole room. 'Some of you may not know that tomorrow's show has a very personal family connection.'

Mimi's stomach dropped to her shoes and she willed him to stop talking. *No.* He could not possibly know who was behind Studio Designs. *Please do not do say another word, Luca; I am begging you. Not now. Not one more word.*

'Tomorrow the fourth generation of Fiorini designers will be presenting her first signature collection. I am sure that it will be a great success. On behalf of the entire Fiorini family, I am delighted to be able to congratulate my dear cousin, Mimi Fiorini Ryan, on her great achievement. It is pleasing to know that a Fiorini is still designing wonderful fashion. *Brava*, Mimi. *Brava*!'

The silence was so thick she could have sliced it. And then the room exploded around her.

She couldn't speak. She had lost sight of Luca from the crush of people around her and the light from camera flashes was blinding her.

Aurelia and her friends were suddenly next to her, chatting furiously about how she was a sly one and asking why she had not told them earlier. Only, as she turned to try and put together some sort of explanation, men in suits started pushing voice recorders into her face and firing questions at her from both sides.

'Mimi! Over here, Mimi.'

'Is that a Fiorini outfit you are wearing?'

'How does it feel to be the next in line to the Fiorini designer crown?'

'Has the family firm helped you put together the collection we are going to see tomorrow?'

'Are you going to head up a new Fiorini line in London?'

'When is the Mimi Ryan Signature Collection coming out in the shops? How long will we have to wait?'

'Just who designed these clothes, Mimi?'

Suddenly a domineering muscular man with a cane pushed the recorders away from Mimi and blocked the reporters from coming any closer.

'That's enough for tonight, guys,' Hal said in a deep, commanding voice which was impossible to argue with. 'We hope to see you all at the fashion show tomorrow. After you've seen Miss Ryan's designs, she will be happy to answer your questions. Thanks. See you at the show tomorrow and enjoy the party.'

Seizing a chance, and while Hal was still occupied with the photographers, Mimi simply turned her back on him and the party and walked as gracefully as she could through the smiling well-wishers towards the exit.

And fled out of the hotel and down the stone steps as fast as she could manage without falling over.

'Mimi. Wait. Please!'

Hal hobbled down the stone steps one at a time, cursing the pain that jetted through his leg as he tried to hurry, and reached the pavement just as Mimi was trying to attract the intention of a passing black taxi-cab.

To his overwhelming relief, her steps slowed.

Mimi turned slowly on the stone pavement and looked back at him, her face contorted with such pain, regret and grief and every kind of emotion he did not want to see there.

She did not speak. She did not need to. Her face told him everything he needed to know.

All of her inner pain, the hurt, the bewilderment and the humiliation were combined into that one single look.

And in that fraction of a second he knew.

He was falling for Mimi Ryan—a woman who he had met only a week ago. A woman who had turned his crazy world upside down and in every direction possible.

He wasn't ready for this. Not now. Not with the turmoil of Tom's death still so raw and whirling around inside his head and heart. He barely knew what day of the week it was. How could he trust his feelings when he still felt so broken and fractured he doubted he could ever be whole again? He couldn't—and it would be totally wrong to tell Mimi how he felt until he had put that past behind him.

But there was one thing he could not hide—her

good opinion mattered. If he only did this one thing, he *had* to tell Mimi the truth and make her understand that he had not betrayed her trust, that he had been as surprised as she had been when Luca Fiorini had walked into the party. Because if he didn't the cost would be too great.

He knew that now. He could *not* lose this girl, no matter what happened between them going forward.

Hal forced his feet to move, hands and cane loose by his sides, aware that Mimi was still standing in silence, just looking at him in disgust and disappointment.

He had to persuade her to listen to him. That was all that mattered.

'I'm so sorry, Mimi. I had no *idea* that Poppy had invited Luca Fiorini tonight. Poppy didn't know anything about your connection to the Fiorini family, and she never intended to upset you. I think Luca saw your photograph in the catalogue and made the connection, but he didn't say a word to Poppy. Please, believe me. I didn't know that Luca was going to be here.'

He stretched out his hand and opened his fingers

for her to take before lowering his voice and trying as best he could to smile and mean it.

'Why don't you come back inside? I am sure that Luca would love to talk to you. We can turn this around and make the best of it. This is your party, your celebration. Please, come back in.'

Mimi looked at him and for a second her chin quivered with emotion before she answered in a low, bitter voice. 'You did not listen to one word I said back in my apartment. Not one! I told you that I wanted nothing to do with the family—this has to be *my* work, my achievement! Not theirs! The only thing waiting for me back inside that room is more humiliation and embarrassment.'

She shook her head slowly from side to side. 'I am not ready to talk to Luca. Not like this. Can't you understand that?'

She was gulping down breaths of air and gesticulating widely, but he had his own response. Fighting to control his voice, he snatched at some small chance to turn this around.

'No. *You* are the one who is not listening to *me*. I didn't know he had been invited. How could I? Poppy must have pulled a lot of strings to persuade the head of a fashion house to turn up in person, but there was no reason for her to tell me about it.'

He took a step closer so they were both at the same height.

'It was *your* decision not to tell Poppy that you were related to the Fiorinis. *Yours.* So do not blame Poppy for inviting as many of her fashion-trade friends as possible to bring in as much publicity as she could for your show. You should be pleased that he is here at all.'

Mimi blinked and looked stunned by his statement, then gesticulated back to the hotel entrance. 'Pleased? Pleased that everyone in the room was staring at me like that?'

She closed her eyes and shook her head. 'Why am I even trying to explain? You obviously have no idea that Luca Fiorini has just ruined every plan I had built up for my career. I wish I had never told you anything about my family.'

'Then why did you? Why *did* you tell me about your dad and your terrible graduation show?'

Mimi glared up at him wide-eyed.

'You know why. And don't you dare try and change the subject.'

'You told me because you thought I would feel

sorry for you, didn't you? The poor schoolgirl who lost her father because the Fiorini family kept him on a string. The cruel words from the rich and famous relatives. Come on, admit it—you wanted my pity!'

Hal reached out and tried to take her arm, but she knocked it aside. 'Go back to Poppy and your mountains, Hal! Go back to your sports and your camera. You don't know anything about me!'

'I know that you've been living in that museum of a shop for the last ten years of your life. Ten years! That's a prison sentence, not a life.'

He took a step closer.

'Don't turn this into one more excuse for locking yourself away and wallowing in your own self-pity. One more excuse for not taking a risk and making a decision about your life. You want to be with me as much as I want to be with you. And do not even try and put the blame on me!'

'Poppy…'

Hal took her hand, firmly this time, and he had no intention of letting it go.

'This is not about Poppy. Or the show. This is about you, Mimi. I'm not listening to any more excuses about your relatives. They won't work this time. And they never did.'

He took another step closer until his face was only inches from hers, his eyes locked onto hers.

'Do you truly want to run back to your safe little flat, above your safe little shop, with the same safe friends? Do you want to spend the rest of your life finding one excuse or another for not taking a chance at happiness, blaming something or someone else for your loneliness? And what happens when you can't afford to keep the shop going? What do you do then?'

Mimi opened her mouth to answer, but instead her lip quivered with emotion and she closed her eyes as his words seemed to hit home.

When he spoke again, his voice was slower, calmer. A whisper. His hand wrapped around her waist, drawing her shaking body into the warmth of his embrace.

'You don't have to live in your family's shadow. You have a choice and I want to help you be the best you can be. You are the most talented woman I have ever met in my life, Mimi. Will you give me a chance to be part of your life? Will you take a risk with me?'

Both of her hands were pressed hard against his dinner suit jacket, and he could only wait, his heart pounding, as she lifted and pressed her palms down again before she was ready to lift her head and look him hard in the eyes.

He didn't like what he saw there.

'How can I? I don't know the first thing about you, Hal. I've told you things about my life and parents which I have never even spoken about before! And what have you told me, shared with me, trusted me with?'

She stared hard and the knot in his stomach grew to epic proportions.

'Nothing. You have not told me one thing that means something to you! Tonight I had to hear from Tom's girlfriend that you were so strong for everyone else after Tom died. How do you think that makes me feel? She assumed that you had told me all about the accident. That's what people do when they are close, they talk about the important things in their life. Well, so far I seem to have been the one doing all of the talking.'

'Aurelia? She told you about that?'

'Oh, yes. Except, of course, she thought I knew all about it. Have you any clue as to what it feels like to be the only person in the room who is not in on some big secret? The outsider? I felt as though everyone in that room knew about Tom's accident except me. Everyone!'

'I'm sorry. I should have told you.'

Mimi pushed hard against his chest with both fists and stepped back, increasing the distance between them in every way possible.

'Yes, you should. And it is way too late now. Oh, Hal! You promised to take care of me. And you *didn't*. You should have told me and you didn't! Why? Why could you not tell me about what happened on the day he died? Do I mean so little to you? Is that it?'

'No. You mean a very great deal to me. But I promised Tom that I wouldn't tell anyone about what happened on the day he died until the time was right. That's why I couldn't tell you the truth. Why I haven't been able to tell anyone the truth. Those people at the party only know that we had a climbing accident. They have no idea about what really happened.'

Her whole body stilled and she turned back to him. 'What do you mean? Why do you have to wait until the time is right? I don't understand.'

Hal froze, his back rigid, and so taut that when he spoke the energy of his words reverberated through his chest and were amplified in the air that separated them.

'Tom was dying of cancer. He didn't go to the mountain to climb that day. He went to the mountain to die the way he wanted to die. And I helped him do it. I helped my best friend kill himself.'

CHAPTER TWELVE

MIMI lost track of time as they walked, slowly, silently, around the park, the distance between them shifting as her feet began to hurt and Hal's cane knocked against a park bench or the trunk of a tree or shrub.

There were no words, no false motivational speeches of consolation or explanation. Simply two people lost in their own worlds and thoughts that happened to be on parallel tracks at the same time.

The gap between them on the narrow path was only a few feet, but she had never felt so distant from another person.

Hal had not tried to hold her hand, or explain.

He had simply followed her into the quiet space in the cool of the late evening, away from the busy street, the noise and bright lights of the smart hotel, and the glittering people within it, who were probably wondering where they had got to. She had walked out of her own pre-show party but she could not think about that now. Hal was all that mattered.

She needed time to calm herself and try and make some sense of what Hal had told her.

He had helped Tom to kill himself? That had to be some sort of horrible, terrible mistake. He had been his friend. He had been going to be the best man at Tom's wedding to Aurelia. No, there was more to this than a simple admission of guilt.

He would tell her when he was ready. If she was willing to listen.

The lovely limo-shoes she had chosen tripped over a pebble on the pavement, hurting her toes, and she flinched and walked gingerly over to a wooden park bench which was half-hidden under the shade of a large tree, set back from the path and surrounded by shrubbery. It was dark, sheltered and secluded. She collapsed down on the rough seat, uncaring now about the damage it would cause to her new dress, and slipped off her shoe so that she could massage her toes.

From her place in the dark she could see Hal walk slowly up the pavement in the faint streetlight until he was only a few feet away from her, but with his head turned away from the light so that she could not see his face. From his stiff back and hunched up shoulders, everything about Hal's body screamed that he was tense and in pain, and she wanted to go to him. And knew that she couldn't.

The physical distance from Hal was nothing compared to the dark, unspoken secrets that kept them apart.

Mimi closed her eyes and breathed in the cool, damp evening air, desperate to calm her reeling brain. He had asked her to give him a chance, to take a risk on him.

Oh, Hal. You ask that and then you hit me with your secret about Tom. What other secrets are weighing you down? How much do I really know about you?

She wondered how long it had been since he had trusted anyone with the truth about who he was and the burdens from the past he was carrying with him.

He had been right to challenge her about her safe little life in her shop and apartment, but at that moment her coping strategies seemed liked nothing compared to the weight of responsibilities and debt that she was carrying.

What was she going to do—walk away? Or stay and help him?

One thing was clear: what happened next was not up to her. It was up to Hal. He had to decide whether he was going to open up his secret world and let her in. Or not. He had turned the key and told her what lay inside. But the door was still firmly closed in her face.

And she was going to stay on this bench, in the dark shadows, until he made the decision.

Minutes stretched out until she could feel the slight damp penetrate her evening jacket and she squeezed her swollen foot back into her shoe, knocking it against the bench as she did so.

That simple movement echoed across the air between them and as she watched Hal from her shadowy seat his shoulders seemed to slump back a little and his voice sounded out across the gloom. It was as wonderful as the first time she had heard it in Poppy's office, but now tinged with deep emotion, which totally captured her attention, forcing her to listen with her whole body.

'Tom was diagnosed with an incurable lymphoma. He had put his muscle weakness down to some horrible virus we picked up on the last tour of Patagonia, but this time it didn't get better. It got worse—bad enough for me to drag him to have tests.'

Hal turned his face a little so she could see that he was staring at the hard stone surface ahead of him, as though trying to gain strength to carry on. But her heart was singing. He was opening up to her—finally!

'The diagnosis still came as a shock. There was nothing they could do. Aggressive treatments would have destroyed his quality of life, so Tom decided to go back to his home in France with Aurelia and enjoy what was left of his life.'

As she looked into his face Hal appeared to falter. Mimi licked her lips and whispered out loud in as gentle a voice as she could manage, 'Did you stay with him? In France?'

Hal twisted his head in her direction then shook it several times. 'I was spending a lot of time with clients in South America, but I got the call about a month later. Tom had spent the winter putting together the charitable foundation for disabled climbers and doing some skiing, but he was losing muscle power faster than he had expected. If we waited much longer he knew he wouldn't be able to make it onto the mountain. So he suggested that we get together for one final trek to check a new walking route in the French Alps for clients. It was probably going to be his last chance for the two of us to go out before he became too weak to make the trip.'

Hal blew out several times. 'I had no idea it was going to be so hard. We had a brilliant few days' holiday, laughing over wonderful food and wine. But that morning we set off after breakfast, and I don't know what it was, but I sensed that something was different.'

He leant on his cane, shifting position. His leg had to be hurting by now, but he did not move on, but braced his cane into the grass.

'It was a beautiful day. Blue sky, warm sunshine reflecting back from the snow cover. I actually felt guilty to be so healthy, alive and well on such a lovely day. After a couple of hours we were the only people on the most dangerous part of the mountain, standing on a narrow ledge, roped together and looking down a sheer rock-face with boulders below us. We hadn't said much on the way up, but suddenly Tom started talking about how he had seen his dad die slowly of cancer when he was a boy and had felt so helpless.'

Hal's fingers tightened, then stretched out and clamped around the cane so fiercely that Mimi could almost see the white of his knuckles.

'He kept telling me there was no way he was prepared to put Aurelia through that agony. He loved her too much for that. So he had decided that when the time was right he would end his life in the mountains. He planned to take back control over his life by deciding how he was going to end it.'

Hal threw back his head against the hard seat. 'You can imagine what I said to that! I even called him a coward, looking for the fast and painless way out, while the rest of us were going to be left behind to pick up the pieces. I didn't want anything to do with it.'

Hal sniffed several times, his head back, and Mimi did not dare look into his face or try and offer words comfort. This was something Hal had to do on his own. He had to survive this.

'I started to get really angry with Tom, calling him all of the selfish names I could think of, begging and pleading with him to think about new treatments which could keep him with us a few more months, or even a year. But Tom had been thinking about the options for weeks. He knew what he was doing.'

Hal wiped his cheek. 'But then he made me promise that I would keep his plan secret so that Aurelia wouldn't know. And it just broke my heart.'

His words came out in shuddering, short breaths. 'He just smiled and hugged me and told me that he was going to miss me. Started talking about all of the crazy mad things we had done together over the years since university, and before long we were both laughing and crying then laughing some more. And then he stopped laughing and said, "tell her when you think the time is right", but he was crying when he said it. It was the first time I had ever seen him cry. And in that fraction of a second, while I was distracted, Tom unclipped the rope holding us together, told me that he loved me, took two steps backwards and fell off the mountain. Onto the rocks below.'

It was no good; Mimi had to go to him. Pushing herself away from the bench, she covered the few feet that separated them and took hold of his right hand in silence.

Mimi had not even realised she had stopped breathing until Hal paused for a second to suck in a lung of cool evening air and she finally had the nerve to look at him. Although his eyes were open, Hal was staring into the branches of the trees above their heads and she could just make out the deep frown lines of his forehead.

'I suppose it was the shock of seeing him go over like that, but a lifetime of instinct kicked in. He was my best friend. He was Tom. I couldn't just let him go; I had to save him. Which is why I lunged after him, trying to grab a hold of him before it was too late.'

Hal looked across at Mimi and gave a slight shrug as she squeezed his hand. 'But I couldn't. The rope wasn't long enough. There wasn't anywhere to place a solid peg, so I took a risk with a small knife-blade pushed into a crack in the face, and prayed that it would take my weight for another few feet. It didn't. And I fell. Some hero, huh?'

'You tried. You should be proud of what you tried to do.'

'Proud? I knew Tom had broken his neck when I was only halfway down. There was nothing I could have done to help him. It was hopeless. I was hopeless.'

Hal slipped his hand from Mimi's fingers and hobbled along the grass, holding on to one tree trunk then another.

'Now do you see why I couldn't tell Aurelia or Poppy or anyone else about my stupid accident? I promised Tom that I would keep his secret. And I have kept my word, even when it was tearing me apart, knowing how much the family he loved were grieving. I tried to take care of them as best I could, but it was so hard. I was in pain. My leg wasn't healing, and all the time all I could think of was what I could have done differently on that day. Every night I go through the same nightmare when I replay in my head the moment he went over the edge. Over and over again. I was so useless; I couldn't even save my friend.'

'Is that why you came back to help raise money for the foundation? To do something positive to remember him?'

He half-turned to Mimi and slowly shook his head from side to side. 'You are a gentle and beautiful soul, but I think you already know that I came back to ease my guilt enough to see me through each day. Believe me, the last thing I want to do is be surrounded by photographs of Tom looking so alive and vibrant. But this is what Tom wanted as his legacy.'

She moved forward and stood in front of him, the palms of her hands pressed flat against his jacket so he was forced to look down into her face. 'Aurelia told me you were a tower of strength to the family after Tom died. But who did *you* confide in, Hal? Who was *your* tower of strength when you needed someone to talk to?'

He slowly shook his head. 'Poppy was great, but there was no one I could really turn to. How could they understand it all when I still don't fully understand it myself?'

'So you took all of that pain inside yourself. Oh, Hal.' She was stroking his face now, her fingers moving back from his still-damp cheeks into his hair. 'Tell me, what do *you* really want to do next with your life?'

He reached up, took her hands, brought them back down to her chest and held them there before taking a long breath. 'What do I want to do? I want to get through the show tomorrow. I want to take some time out to see what my smashed ankle can do and then maybe, if I am lucky, I can rebuild some sort of photographic career for myself away from high-risk sports. But it is going to be very tough.'

A sweet smile flashed across his lips and he released one hand long enough to touch the tip of her nose. 'Any jobs going in your knitting shop? You are going to need someone to sell the yarn while you build up your fashion-design empire.'

Mimi smiled back at him and sighed out loud. 'Hal! Stop trying to change the subject. You already have a perfectly good job at Langdon Events. And in your spare time you seem to enjoy pointing a camera at people.'

She swallowed down a moment of fear than spoke her mind. 'You should make that documentary about Tom. Aurelia deserves to hear the truth about the sacrifice he made—the sacrifice you both made. Will you think about it? Please? Otherwise I don't know how I am going to get through tomorrow, with the two of you standing so close but with this massive secret creating a barrier between you.'

Hal gasped. 'You can't tell her,' he rushed out. 'You can't tell anyone about Tom. Promise me, Mimi. This has to stay a secret between us.'

She listened to the sound of their breathing before shaking her head slowly from side to side. 'No, Hal. I found out tonight that family secrets don't stay hidden no matter how hard you want them to. Aurelia is probably still in the party with Poppy. Now would seem as good a time as any. And this is something only you can do.'

Mimi slowly, slowly slid her body out of the warm arms of this remarkable man who had been through so much and felt bereft the instant she broke away from his touch.

'I can get home on my own. You have things to do before I see you tomorrow.'

And with that she turned her back on him so that he would not see her tears and walked slowly away from him, back into the real world of the street on the other side of the park and a black taxi-cab.

Mimi stretched out in her bed as the early-morning sunlight peeked in around the edges of her flowery bedroom curtains, snuggled down farther under the duvet and tried to find a comfortable spot on her pillow.

Only she couldn't because she was still wearing her pearls from the night before—which had left their mark on her neck—and what was left of her make-up, which had left its mark on the pillow.

And she didn't care.

Hal's revelation about the sacrifice his friend had made for those he'd loved had hit her hard, like a tornado whirling around inside her head all night.

Because she had woken up with a muzzy head and one single, burning, crystal-clear thought.

She was not going to allow the Fiorini family to taint her first chance to show what she was capable of. Not now. *Not ever.*

From the moment when Luca Fiorini had declared to the party guests that she was the fourth generation of Fiorini designers, everything changed, and there was nothing that she could do to turn back time and cancel that out. The deed was done and she was going to have to work with that fact and get on with her life.

Her mind had been such a whirlwind on the taxi journey home that she had longed for the calm, peaceful sanctuary of the shop and apartment where she had made her home.

Except that by the time she had collapsed through her door the telephone had been ringing off the hook with calls from the press, friends and TV companies, the voice mail was full and in the end she had pulled the cord out of the wall so she could actually fall into an exhausted but restless sleep.

All night long one thing that her cousin Luca had said had rattled around inside her brain as she tossed and turned. He had congratulated her on her 'first signature collection'.

Interesting idea. But why not go all the way and call it the *Mimi Ryan* Signature Collection? Drat Luca for being a better businessman than she was. If that was what a lifetime of marketing a brand brought to the table, then she would take that crumb of an idea and go with it as some vague repayment for the past.

Not Mimi *Fiorini* Ryan. That would never happen. But if people associated her work with the Fiorini family then she would have to live with that and be honest and open.

Hal had been right to challenge her about the

reason for her decision not to tell anyone that she was a member of the Fiorini family.

Life truly was too short to limit herself because of the past.

Well, that was about to change. If Luca was at the show later then she would deal with that as one professional to another. Who knew? She might even like him!

Little wonder her brain was buzzing with new goals and a new direction.

So, thank you, cousin Luca, for giving me the idea. Now all she had to do was create a brand-new business and work with all of the determination she had left to make the Mimi Ryan Signature Collection a reality so she could promote it at the show.

Which was only a few short hours away.

Mimi pulled the pillow out from under her head and dropped it over her face, groaning out loud in despair.

She should be thanking Hal. Thanking him for trusting her with the secret he had been carrying about Tom's death.

And what about thanking Hal for asking her to take a risk with him?

Oh, Hal!

The pillow slid down from her face, dragging what was left of her make-up with it.

She would have to see Hal again and work with him to make the show a success to the public, not just the professionals. But how was she going to face him?

He probably would not want to talk to her—not after what she had said last night as they'd parted.

After everything they had shared these past few days, after she had become so accustomed to the sound of his voice and the touch of his lips on her skin, after all of their hard work, she needed to share this special day with him. No matter what happened going forward.

Her throat tightened and she brushed away a treacherous slick of moisture from the corner of each eye. Flinging back the covers, she winced at the twisted mess that had been her best lingerie and sighed with pleasure as she recalled Hal's touch, the way his fingers had smoothed over her stomach when he had helped her out of her corset.

A shiver ran across her body and she gulped down the memory. Whatever happened between them over the next few days, she was going to live with the memory of these last days with Hal as some of the best of her life.

She blinked and sat up slowly, saw her reflection in the mirror and winced, before touching two fingers to her pearls in a small salute to the girl with terrible bed-hair looking back at her.

Only forward. She had a lot of work to do today and she needed to get on and do it.

Only forward, indeed.

An hour later she was showered, make-up free and in the studio working at her PC with tea and toast to add extra fuel to the driving ambition. She was just thinking through a design for the company logo for 'Mimi Ryan Signature Designs' when the doorbell to the shop rang.

She was already out of her chair and moving before her feet slowed; she did not usually have customers at dawn on a Saturday morning.

It had to be the media wanting an interview—or Hal.

Perhaps he had come over to talk things through. It had to be him; nobody else would be crazy enough to turn up at this time of the morning.

Shuffling forward a little at a time, Mimi peeked through the studio door so she could see what was happening at the front of the shop, then looked again. There was nobody there.

Fighting back, and cursing herself for, a crushing sense of disappointment that it was not Hal, Mimi strolled to the door and opened it just wide enough to have a look outside.

Just as she was about to go back inside, her eye caught a brightly coloured package which had been left on the door step.

With a wry smile she bent down, swooped up the heavy package from her step and peeked inside. Her senses reeled as the intensely sweet aroma of white jasmine flowers filled her nose.

It was a living plant inside a beautiful, hand-decorated ceramic pot which would be a perfect match to the one on her patio.

Hal!

She glanced around the quiet early-morning street, her heart thumping, but there was no sign of anyone. Stepping backwards, still looking around in case she missed him, Mimi closed the front door and carried the jasmine back into her studio.

As she carefully pulled away the bright wrapping paper her fingers connected with a padded envelope which had been crudely taped to the side of the pot.

She inhaled deeply and opened the package. There was a plastic case with a DVD inside. And a piece of the wrapping paper which had been roughly torn from the roll so he could write a note on the back of it.

Oh, yes; that was Hal.

Trying to ignore her trembling fingers, Mimi unfurled the scroll of paper and read the few words he had scribbled in a fast hand:

I'm sorry for being too much of a coward to tell you my sordid past. I was way too scared that you would throw me if you knew what kind of a loser I was. Thank you for listening last night. And the camera never lies, Mimi. I love who you are, and you are beautiful. Question is, are you willing to take a chance on me?

Hal.

The camera never lies? He loves who I am? Oh, what had he done now?

Hardly daring to look at the monitor, Mimi

slipped the DVD into her computer and clicked on the icon for the photos.

Bright colour photographs slid across the screen. There were dozens of them.

The art gallery; Mimi joking with some of the students, adding a crystallised flower to one of the tea-service cupcakes.

The studio; she was working on some extra embroidery on the sleeve of a jacket, her face creased and muscles straining with the total focus she was giving to the work.

A close-up of her working with Lola at the hotel, laughing with her head back in the sunlit elegance of that stunning room. Altering the hem on her blue dress with pins in her mouth.

All the time there were close-up shots of her neck, wrists, face and hair; details of the way she held a needle and the way her head dropped back when she laughed.

Her smile. Her sad face. Her tired, pale, drawn face.

She had not even realised that she leant forward when she spoke to a student.

But Hal had noticed it. He had been watching

her from behind the camera lens. And he had been taking her photograph all week.

He loved who she was.

'Oh, Hal,' she said out loud.

There was a faint rustling noise behind her back, and she glanced behind her—to see Hal, standing on the patio, one hand in his pocket, the other resting on his cane. Just watching her. He looked exhausted, with a stubbly chin; his lovely dinner suit was grimy and crumpled. *Perfection!*

She looked into his face—and her heart broke.

She ran as fast as her legs could carry her to the patio and flung herself into his open arms, squealing, laughing and crying with happiness as he hoisted her from around the waist, hugged her and hugged her again in the sunshine, his bright laughter joining hers.

Mimi tried to answer, but her throat was too tight, the tears running down her cheeks.

When he spoke again, his voice was slower, calmer; a whisper. His forehead was pressed against hers, and his hand wrapped around her waist, drawing her shaking body into the warmth of his embrace.

'You weren't answering the phone so I had to

come in through the back gate. Let me into your life, Mimi. Will you do that? Let me love you?'

Her response was to take his face between her cupped hands, close her eyes and kiss him long enough and lovingly enough to leave them both breathless.

'Yes. Yes, Hal. I don't need a camera and a photo collection to know that I love who you are. I understand who you are and I need to be with you.'

'Does that mean I can keep my sleeping bag here permanently?' he asked between kisses.

And that really did make her laugh. Mimi moved forward to kiss Hal very gently on the lips, safe inside the circle of his arms.

'No more sleeping bags. Not any more. This is your home from now on. If you want it?'

'More than anything. It's time for this old soul to put down some roots, and there is nowhere else I want to be. I took your advice, by the way, which is why I have been awake all night.'

Her breath caught in her throat. 'You told Aurelia.'

He nodded. 'I asked Aurelia to come back to Poppy's place after the party and I told them *everything*. And I mean everything! There were lots of tears, some laughter and then more tears, but they know the truth and that's a start. Aurelia still wants to work on the documentary about Tom, and I've agreed to do it as soon as I am fit enough.'

'Oh, Hal, that's amazing. I am so proud of you.'

'And what about you? What do you want to do now?' he asked, his smiling eyes never leaving her face as his long fingers cupped her chin and gently wiped away her tears of happiness with his thumbs.

'Apart from loving you? Oh, I thought I might launch a brand-new company making ready-to-wear designs right here in my studio and sold through department stores. I will need to ask Poppy for help with introductions to people who can source materials and create the perfect website before making any decisions. Then I have to find investors and make samples for fashion buyers and the like.' Mimi stroked his hair back from his forehead as he looked into her face.

'Still the entrepreneur?' he asked, trying not to laugh.

'Absolutely. I am thinking of "Mimi Ryan Signature Designs".' Her hand lifted and she wrote the name in the air in large scrolling letters, testing it for size before smiling at Hal. 'What do you think?'

'I love it. There is no way you are going to get rid of me, young lady,' Hal answered, his voice soft and caring. 'You should know by now that the Langdon men are very hard to shake off. I talked to Poppy this morning and told her that I am officially reporting for duty in the London office for the next twelve months so I can focus on getting better while getting under her feet on a daily basis.'

'Is that what you truly want, Hal?' Mimi asked as he lowered her to the patio stones, begging him to say yes. She took both of Hal's hands in hers as he nodded. 'Be honest. Don't you want to go back to France?'

'France is my past and London my future. I might have a few things to learn about wedding planning, but it would do me good to be in one place for more than a few weeks at a time. Poppy has managed the company on her own long enough, and I can run the sports projects through the Internet from anywhere in the world. But that's next week. Right now we have a fashion show to put on, young lady.'

'Which means we need to get busy. There's a lot to sort out in the next—' she glanced down at her watch '—six hours. And then I am thinking of braving a holiday outside London, but I shall need a guide. Do you know anyone who might be available?'

'Just tell me and I'll take you anywhere you want to go. Anywhere. I am going to be around for quite a while.' He smiled with such love in his eyes as his fingers lovingly caressed the back of her head. 'I know a great hotel in the mountains in Japan which would be perfect for you.'

'Japan? Oh, that would be amazing. But first...' Mimi looked over his shoulder then tilted her head to wink at him. 'I thought I might start my adventures with that guided tour behind the screen—if it's not too much trouble?'

*London Chronicle, Fashion Week
special supplement, June 2010*

NEW LONDON DESIGNER SELLS ENTIRE DEBUT COLLECTION

Local designer Mimi Ryan delighted the audience with her debut fashion show on Saturday in aid of the Tom Harris Foundation for Climbing for the Disabled.

The show was introduced by Luca Fiorini of the couture-house Fiorini International who, in a rare public appearance, praised the workmanship, elegance and stunning design of the Mimi Ryan Signature Collection. Following the show, Mr Fiorini personally introduced Miss Ryan to many of the fashion buyers at the show and later that evening, at a prestigious party he had arranged in her honour.

In a statement to the press, Miss Ryan confirmed that she had sold her entire ready-to-wear collection of women's clothing to an international retailer and the spring-summer designs would be available in luxury department stores worldwide early next year.

Media coverage of this charity event was provided by the award-winning sports photographer Hal Langdon, of Langdon Events, who is preparing to film a documentary about the late mountaineer Tom Harris. It is understood that Mr Langdon will be accompanying Miss Ryan on her overseas visits to meet buyers over the next few months, beginning with an extended holiday in Japan and the Far East.

* * * * *

MILLS & BOON PUBLISH EIGHT
LARGE PRINT TITLES A MONTH.
THESE ARE THE TITLES FOR SEPTEMBER 2011.

ೞ

TOO PROUD TO BE BOUGHT
Sharon Kendrick

A DARK SICILIAN SECRET
Jane Porter

PRINCE OF SCANDAL
Annie West

THE BEAUTIFUL WIDOW
Helen Brooks

RANCHER'S TWINS: MUM NEEDED
Barbara Hannay

THE BABY PROJECT
Susan Meier

SECOND CHANCE BABY
Susan Meier

HER MOMENT IN THE SPOTLIGHT
Nina Harrington

Mills & Boon® Large Print
October 2011

PASSION AND THE PRINCE
Penny Jordan

FOR DUTY'S SAKE
Lucy Monroe

ALESSANDRO'S PRIZE
Helen Bianchin

MR AND MISCHIEF
Kate Hewitt

HER DESERT PRINCE
Rebecca Winters

THE BOSS'S SURPRISE SON
Teresa Carpenter

ORDINARY GIRL IN A TIARA
Jessica Hart

TEMPTED BY TROUBLE
Liz Fielding

0911 Rom LP

Discover Pure Reading Pleasure with

Visit the Mills & Boon website for all the latest in romance

- **Buy** all the latest releases, backlist and eBooks

- **Find out** more about our authors and their books

- **Join** our community and chat to authors and other readers

- **Free** online reads from your favourite authors

- **Win** with our fantastic online competitions

- **Sign** up for our free monthly eNewsletter

- **Tell us** what you think by signing up to our reader panel

- **Rate** and review books with our star system

www.millsandboon.co.uk

 Follow us at twitter.com/millsandboonuk

 Become a fan at facebook.com/romancehq